KT-134-525

THE SINFUL ART OF REVENGE

BY

MAYA BLAKE

First published in Great Britain 2013
by Mills & Boon, an imprint of Harlequin (UK) Limited.
Harlequin (UK) Limited, Eton House, 18-24 Paradise Road,
Richmond, Surrey TW9 1SR

© Maya Blake 2013

ISBN: 978 0 263 90001 9

Harlequin (UK) policy is to use papers that are natural, renewable and recyclable products and made from wood grown in sustainable forests. The logging and manufacturing process conform to the legal environmental regulations of the country of origin.

Printed and bound in Spain
by Blackprint CPI, Barcelona

THE SINFUL ART OF REVENGE

CHAPTER ONE

AFTER THREE HUNDRED YARDS, turn right.

Damion Fortier ignored the sultry voice of his satellite navigator and accelerated his Bugatti Veyron past the floodlit tree-lined lane that led to Ashton Manor. The aging Duke he'd liberally plied with Krug and caviar all evening at his exclusive London private gentlemen's club had supplied Damion with directions to a less well-known entrance to Sir Trevor Ashton's Surrey country residence—one Damion fully intended to use.

Turn around when possible.

The veiled reproach barely registered. A quarter of a mile up the road he slowed down and turned into a narrower lane. Ahead of him he could see the rear of the aging Manor. The gardens on this side of the estate were remarkably less manicured than the showcased frontage cultivated to fool the less discerning. With an impatient hand he shut off the navigator's repeated entreaty to turn around. He had reached his destination.

Satisfaction oozed through him even as confusion threaded doubt through his mind. Considering the money he'd spent to achieve what he wanted, this whole situation should have gone much more smoothly. He'd learnt very early on in life that some people responded only to cold, hard cash, and he'd expected it this time, too.

But his investigators had already been to Ashton Manor once before and been stonewalled. Which was unacceptable.

He stopped the car at the bottom of the back garden and stepped out.

Annoyance made his movements jerky as he climbed the stone steps and approached the ivy-trellised Manor. Despite being cloaked by the inky-black night, its dilapidated status couldn't be hidden.

As he drew nearer he heard female laughter, interlaced with several deeper tones. He skirted a bramble-choked rosebush and felt it snag on his trouser leg. Jaw tightening, he stared down at his ruined trousers.

He reached down to free himself and hissed with anger when a thorn bit into his thumb.

Pressing his tongue to the torn flesh to stem the blood flow, Damion stepped up to the tall double windows of the Georgian mansion. Several couples stood outside the drawing room, preparing to take their leave. It was obvious they'd been partying a while; one or two of them weren't quite steady on their feet.

Damion scanned the crowd but didn't immediately spot her.

He stepped back onto the overgrown path, abandoning his previous intention of stealth. About to stalk round to the front of the Manor, Damion paused as a figure nudged into his peripheral vision.

Her presence was unobtrusive, her movements graceful, unhurried, intended not to draw attention to herself. And yet as if drawn by her magnetism, the group turned at her approach.

The light from the room spilled over her. The air snagged mid-breath in Damion's chest and his whole body clenched in remembrance.

On any other woman the white kimono-style gown that lightly hugged her body would have looked simple and elegant— sexy but not sexual.

But on her the body-skimming design immediately drew the eye to her plump breasts, the tiny indentation of her cinched-in waist and the voluptuous curve of her hips. Damion followed the flow of the silk dress. If his memory served him right, she would either be wearing a very tiny thong or nothing at all underneath that silk.

Recalling her proclivity for designer thongs—and how he'd been obsessed with taking them off—he felt a pulse of heat shoot through him, surprising him with it intensity.

His frowning gaze rose to her face. She wore her hair differently now. A heavy fringe slanted over one temple, covering most of the right side of her face, while the rest of her long, dark hair hung thick and luxurious down her back. Her make-up was a little more on the heavy, dramatic side than he remembered her favouring, but even without those camouflaging accessories Damion recognised her immediately.

Reiko Kagawa.

The woman he'd been hunting for weeks. The woman who'd become so skilled in camouflage and subterfuge she'd eluded his security experts. And almost eluded him, too, save for a chance conversation with a drunken duke...

Damion's gaze travelled over her as she moved through the small gathering. She was still a strikingly beautiful woman... if you preferred your women pocket-Venus-size and duplicitous to the core.

People changed. He knew that. Hell, the five years since he'd last seen Reiko had taught him fresh life lessons he would willingly unlearn. But he'd never thought *she* would end up this way...

The epitome of all he despised.

Tightening his fist, he reminded himself of why he was here—because of his grandfather, the last of his blood relatives. The only one he cared enough about to put himself through this...

Damion refused to let heartache linger at the thought of what lay ahead. He would do what needed to be done for his grandfather, regardless of the personal cost to himself. Five years had passed since he'd set eyes on Reiko—five years since he'd learned that the woman he'd thought he knew was just an aberration.

This time he had his eyes wide open. And once he had what he wanted, she could go back to being a minor blip in his past.

Rounding the old Manor, he marched up the front steps.

A shiver raced down Reiko's spine a split second before the knock came. She tore her gaze from the window, where it had swung as if compelled by an unknown force.

For several moments her mind remained blank, a whisper of premonition shivering over her skin as she glanced back at the tall windows. There was nothing out there except overgrown bushes and the odd fox or two.

Yet…

The knock sounded again, followed almost immediately by the pull of the ancient doorbell no one used much any more.

Recalling that she'd sent Simpson, the day butler, home, Reiko put down the loaded tray she'd been carrying and headed towards the door. The party had been a bad idea. The financial strain alone didn't bear thinking about. But Trevor had insisted.

To keep up appearances.

Her lips twisted. She knew all about keeping up appearances; she had a master's degree in it, in fact. When she needed to, like tonight, she could smile, laugh, negotiate her way through tricky conversation, while desperately keeping a lid on the demons that strained at the leash just below the surface.

The façade was cracking. Nowadays even the little effort it took to smile drained her. And it had all started since she'd heard *he* was looking for her…

Her thoughts skated to a halt as the door flew open. The hundred-year-old oak, worn from lack of proper care, stood little chance of avoiding a collision with the stone wall.

Reiko gasped at the huge figure filling the doorway.

'There you are.' The deep, velvety voice oozed satisfaction and barely suppressed anger.

'Do you always crash your way into people's homes like some wannabe action hero?' she fired back, despite her thundering heart.

She'd feared this moment would come ever since she'd heard on the grapevine he was looking for her. That was why she never stayed in the same place for more than a few days.

A thick wave of panic rolled over her as she stared at him.

The unmistakable French accent and the air of brutal self-assuredness hadn't lessened since she'd last clapped eyes on

Damion Fortier. If anything, time had added a maturity and depth to the sexy, charismatic man recently polled by French *Vogue* as the most eligible bachelor in the western hemisphere— possibly the whole frickin' world.

The Sixth Baron of St Valoire, descended from a pure line of French aristocracy, was six-foot-four-inches of swoon-worthy masculine beauty—even when in the grip of bristling fury.

Wavy hair the colour of dark chocolate grew long enough to touch the collar of his bespoke grey suit without looking un- kempt or unfashionable. Broad shoulders, honed to perfection during his rugby-playing late teens and early twenties, moved restlessly, drawing attention to their sheer width and power. But, as arresting as his body was, it was his face that captured her attention.

Reiko's art-steeped heritage, cultivated since birth and sharp- ened by years of apprenticeship under her late grandfather's keen tutelage, meant she could spot a true masterpiece from twenty feet—it was, after all, the reason she'd chosen her spe- cialised profession.

Damion Fortier was the epitome of Michelangelo's *David*, his face hauntingly beautiful and yet so uniquely mysterious it drew attention and held it, commanding eyes to worship it.

As for *his* eyes…

They always reminded her of furious storm clouds right be- fore thunder boomed and lightning struck. Or right before—

'Aren't you going to say hello, Reiko?'

Reiko sucked in a long breath to calm her galloping heart- beat. And another in order to find the Zen she needed to deal with the situation.

Despite the colossal trepidation accelerating through her body, she forced herself to move towards him, hand out- stretched. 'Hello… Wait—shall I call you Monsieur Fortier, or do you prefer Baron?'

Without waiting, she took his hand in hers.

Face your demons—wasn't that what her therapist had told

her? If she hadn't been so desperate to stay hidden, Reiko would have called her to demand her money back because so far her advice hadn't worked. If anything, the demons had grown larger.

An explosion of heat shattered her thoughts as Damion's firm fingers curled around hers. Stormy sensation fired up deeply suppressed memories, unnerving her much more than she'd expected. Desperately ignoring it, she covered their entwined hands with her other hand.

Surprise flared in his eyes at her action, as she'd known it would. Her recently learned trick always surprised when she made the bold move. Normally it disarmed long enough for her to read her opponent, to see behind the façade to the real person beneath the civilised gloss. Because, inevitably, there was *always* something else underneath.

'I'd like to be sure of the correct way to address you, since Daniel Fortman is clearly no longer an option.'

Reiko was unprepared for the stab of pain that lanced through her. She'd thought she was over this—had thought five years was enough to get over Daniel…Damion's betrayal.

But then how *could* she forget? She'd watched her grandfather wither away before her eyes, his devastation complete after Damion Fortier had been done with him.

She tried to free her fingers but he'd recovered quickly. 'What the hell do you want?' she said.

His eyes gave nothing away as he used his controlling grasp to push her back one step and nudge the door shut behind him.

'You never gave me a chance to explain—'

'When should I have let you explain? *After* your bodyguards nearly flattened my grandfather's cabin because they thought you'd been kidnapped? Or *after* your head of security inadvertently revealed that far from the casual business acquaintance I believed you to be you were in fact *Damion Fortier*—French royalty, and the man who was ruthlessly ruining the grandfather while sleeping with the granddaughter?' Pain stabbed deeper, reminding her just how blind and trusting she'd been.

'*Sleeping* is a very loose term, since we hardly did any in those six weeks.' His smile held a hint of flint. 'And what happened with your grandfather was just business—'

'Don't you dare try to justify it as *just business*! You took away everything he'd ever worked for, everything that mattered to him. Just so you could fatten your already bloated bank balance.'

Damion shrugged. 'He made a deal, Reiko. Then proceeded to make very bad decisions, which he tried to cover up. Because of his friendship with my grandfather, he was given more than enough time to fix the problem. He didn't. I kept my identity a secret because I didn't want things to get sentimental and messy.'

'Of course. Sentiment is so inconvenient when it comes to making money, isn't it? Do you know my grandfather died barely a month after you bankrupted him?' To this day, she couldn't get over the guilt of not seeing what was going on under her nose until it was too late. She'd been too besotted, too trusting. And she'd paid dearly.

Damion's eyes darkened and his grip tightened around hers. 'Reiko—'

'Can you cut to the chase, please, Baron? I'm sure you didn't pursue me for weeks just to reminisce about the past.' A past she never thought of during her wakeful hours but which had recently blended itself into her nightmares.

His eyes narrowed. 'You knew I was looking for you?'

Reiko forced a smile despite the fresh wave of anxiety that coursed through her. 'Of course. It's been fun watching your security experts' antics. They even came close a few times— Honduras especially.'

'You think this is a game?'

Her heart clenched. 'I have no idea what *this* is. The sooner you enlighten me, the sooner you can get out of my life.'

He seemed lost for several seconds, his gaze lightening then darkening as it scoured her face. Finally his lips firmed, as if he wanted to stem what he was about to say.

'I need you.'

Reiko stared blankly, tried very hard not to swallow, sure he'd see her unease in that simple act. But it was hard not to. 'You…need…me?'

In all the feverish scenarios she'd enacted, this hadn't even occurred to her. After all, what could Damion Fortier possibly want with *her*, after using and discarding her like a piece of garbage?

His grip altered, and the slide of his palm against hers sent another pulse of heat up her arm. Reiko glanced down at their entwined hands and felt a knot tighten in her belly. This hadn't been such a bright idea after all. Rather than throwing him off guard, *she* felt at a disadvantage.

'Let me rephrase that. I need your *expertise*.'

That was more like it. 'Careful, Baron, your sneer isn't exactly endearing. It's taken you weeks to find me. The least you can do is be civil. Otherwise next time I may not be so easy to find.'

'For that to happen I'd have to let you out of my sight. And I have no intention of doing so. As for being civil—I must admit that's a little lower on my list right at this moment.'

She shrugged. 'Well, you can leave, or I can call the police and have you arrested for trespass.'

Intense eyes narrowed. 'That would be a mistake.'

Her smile widened. 'I'm quite happy to let them decide.'

Without releasing her, he extracted his BlackBerry from his pocket and held it out to her. '*Bien sûr*—make the call.'

Despite her smile staying put, she shuddered. The police were the last people she wanted to be dealing with. 'You don't mean that.'

'I'm prepared to accept a charge for trespass. Are *you* prepared for me to hand over the interesting facts I've gathered on you to them?'

Her fingers jerked within his grasp. To cover the telling reaction, she pressed her palm closer to his. His eyes widened,
the grey darkening a touch as his gaze dropped to their entwined fingers.

Despite everything screaming at her to run in the opposite
direction, Reiko went one better. Reaching out, she clasped his
elbow. His head jerked up, his gaze snagging and holding hers
prisoner, his brow furrowing in an attempt to read her.

Sensory overload warred with anxiety. This close to his overwhelming masculinity, she could smell the crisp tones of his
aftershave, along with the heat coming off his toned skin. Frantically she tried to stem the memory of how his skin had felt
against hers, how she'd loved to wear his shirt, roll around in
his scent like some loved-up puppy.

But all she could compute was how perfectly sculpted his
cheekbones were, how lush and damned sexy his spiky lashes
looked, sweeping down to rake over her.

Beneath her dress, her body reacted. A slow burn started
in her stomach, and grew, spreading fiery sensation…taunting
her—

The sound of breaking glass made her jump.

Damion raised an eyebrow.

'The caterers are still here. Give me a few minutes to dismiss them, then you can resume threatening me.'

Eyes narrowed in suspicion, he released her.

Reiko headed for the kitchen, not at all surprised when he
fell into step beside her. She forced herself not to rub her hands
against her thighs to alleviate their intense tingling.

After making sure they hadn't broken a priceless heirloom,
she signed the cheque, thanked and dismissed the catering crew.

Slowly retracing her steps, she carefully altered her walk to
adjust to the pain shooting through her hips and pelvis. She'd
been on her feet for too long in heels far too uncomfortable for
her injuries. But, as much as she wanted to trudge her weary

body upstairs, stretch through her painful exercises before showering for bed, she couldn't give in.

She had to deal with the ex-lover who prowled like a dangerous jungle animal beside her. Straightening her spine, she led him to the living room.

'Right, are you going to resume your ogre impression?' She glanced over at him and caught the edge of bleakness that shot across his face.

He gave a grim smile. 'I'd like to return to London tonight, so I'll get to the point. My grandfather disposed of a collection of three paintings four years ago, shortly after my grandmother died. I believe you know something about them?'

Her chest tightened. 'Maybe.'

His jaw tightened so hard and for so long she feared it would crack. Then he sighed, and she caught the edge of weariness in the sound. 'Don't play games with me, Reiko. I know you were the broker.'

'But games are what we do best—aren't they, *Daniel*? Pretending to be one thing when we're something else?'

He shoved a hand through his hair. 'Look, I was surprised when your grandfather didn't recognise me—'

'He had other things on his mind, like trying to stop you from taking everything away from him.'

Damion nodded. 'Once I realised that, I thought it would be better if he didn't know.'

'And what about me? We were together for six weeks. You could've come clean at any time. You chose not to.' Because she hadn't been important enough—hadn't been worthy of his honesty even after he'd taken her to his bed.

He inhaled sharply. 'Don't over-dramatise what happened between us, Reiko. If I recall, you were surprisingly easy to get rid of. But then you had incentive, didn't you?'

'If you're talking about the money—'

'The money *and the lover who replaced me before the bed was cold*!'

His teeth visibly clenched over the words and a flash of ice washed over her.

Amid the dark panic and unwanted feelings flooding her, shame threaded its way through. It was no use telling herself she had nothing to be ashamed of. She'd let herself down, and it was yet another thing the demons never let her forget.

As she watched, Damion reined his emotions in. But even from across the room she could feel the pulse of his anger and contempt.

'Now that we've relived fond memories, let's move on, shall we?' he said. 'I've retrieved the *Femme de la Voile*. I haven't been able to trace the *Femme en Mer* or the *Femme sur Plage*. It's imperative that I find them both, but *Sur Plage* is the one I want found soonest.'

She forced herself back to the present. 'You want the *Femme en Mer*, too?' she murmured. 'I thought—'

'You thought what?'

Somehow she'd expected Damion Fortier would want to reclaim the largest, most spectacular of the three paintings, not the smallest, the one only a handful of people had been allowed to see in its fifty years in existence.

'Never mind. Why do you want them back?'

He shoved a hand deep into one trouser pocket, a look passing through his eyes that intrigued her.

'That is not your concern.'

He didn't know how wrong he was. 'But it is. You want it for your VIP-only exhibition at Gallerie Fortier in Paris next week. That's why you've been hunting the paintings these past months, isn't it?'

He stilled. 'Only six people are aware of my exhibition. The invitations haven't even gone out yet. How did you come by this information?'

Reiko shrugged. 'I could tell you, but I'd have to kill you. And all that blood would ruin my dress. Pointless, really.'

He sucked in an inflamed breath, then moved so quickly

and silently she barely had time to register his intention before he'd caught her shoulders in a firm grip. 'Who told you about the exhibition?' he demanded.

She held her ground, despite the fire burning through her veins. 'You don't have to worry that I'll leak the information. I never reveal my sources. In my line of business it's suicide.'

'It'll be first degree murder if you don't tell me.'

Reiko held very still, acutely aware that if his left hand dropped one inch lower he'd feel the rough edge of the scar on her arm. 'Wouldn't murder taint your precious family history? Did you know there's a blog dedicated to tracing and record-ing every good deed your family has performed in the last five hundred years? If it's to be believed, no Fortier has so much as stolen a sip of water throughout your glorious generations. Now here you are, threatening murder. Aren't you afraid your ances-tors will return to haunt you if you break tradition?'

His grip tightened. 'I'm prepared to make an exception this once.'

The rigidity in his body, the cold bite of anger in his voice made her think he probably would, too.

'Ah, but with me dead you'd never see your precious paint-ings again.'

A frown gradually darkened his face as his eyes bored into hers. 'I don't remember you being this bitter or twisted five years ago. What the hell has happened to you?'

The observation, coming out of nowhere, sent a thunderbolt of panic coursing through her.

What the hell has happened to you?

Only Trevor and her mother knew what had happened. Trevor would never betray her trust, and her mother was too self-centred to dwell for too long on her daughter's emotional state.

With a forceful wrench, she freed herself from Damion's grasp and gathered every last ounce of willpower to cling to the outward composure she'd battled so damned hard for this past year. The demons she battled in private were another matter.

After taking a few control-installing breaths, she faced him.

'I'm no longer the wide-eyed, gullible puppy you knew five years ago, Baron. So if you've come here hoping I'll happily wag my tail and pant with yearning for you, you're sorely mistaken.'

Damion stared into her perfectly made-up face. Two emotions—surprise and an unacceptable degree of surrealism—twisted through him. His gaze dropped to her lips, to the tiny dark mole above her upper lip. For a single uncontrolled moment he wasn't sure whether he wanted to kiss her or to shake her—another alien concept that added to the absurdity of the situation.

The Reiko he'd known five years ago would have seen her effect on him. She'd have smiled the smile of a shameless temptress then proceeded to taunt him with her body, confident of the inevitable outcome.

This Reiko stared stonily back at him, her gaze dark and hostile, as if she were counting the minutes until he removed himself from her presence.

Damion wasn't prepared for the hollow feeling the observation left inside him.

'I never thought of you as a puppy. Feline and exceptionally cunning with it is a far more accurate description. Knowing what I do about your shady dealings, I suspect that trait has come in handy in your profession.'

'There's nothing underhand about what I do—'

'What about your penchant for handling stolen goods? Goods that more often than not disappear before the authorities are notified of their whereabouts?'

Her pert nose wrinkled in distaste. 'You shouldn't believe everything you read in your fancy art journals.'

'My sources are completely trustworthy.'

'If they were, you wouldn't have wasted your time coming here today. They'd have told you I'm no longer actively involved in the art-retrieval business. I haven't been for the past eighteen months.'

Her brittle tone, the way she hugged her elbows and held herself rigidly, told him there was something more going on here. But weariness dug behind his eyes, bit into his soul, dulled his senses.

For a single heartbeat Damion contemplated walking away, finding another way to appease his grandfather. The thought dissolved before it was fully formed.

Fortier curse or not, he would honour his grandfather's wish—even if it meant dallying with the woman who stared at him with eyes that dared and detested him at the same time. A woman who'd proved herself as faithless as his mother and grandmother.

He gritted his teeth as a flash of guilt seared his mind.

He was here today because he'd walked away from his family, from his duty, for a whole year. In his attempt to escape the stark reality of the obsessive compulsion that dogged his family, he'd walked straight into the arms of the very chaos he'd been trying to escape—and destroyed lives in the process. Never again.

Resolve firmed. 'You'll find the paintings for me.'

Hazel eyes snapped fire at him. 'You order me about as if you own me. You don't, so drop the attitude.'

He allowed himself a whisper of a smile. He now understood why, for such a diminutive figure, her reputation seemed larger than life. She'd obviously developed a blatant disregard for sense or self-preservation.

'I think there's been a misunderstanding, *ma belle*,' he said in a softer, more conversational tone. 'You seem to be labouring under the impression that you can bargain with me. But understand this—you'll use all your resources to find the paintings for me or I *will* hand my dossier over to Interpol. Let them decide what to do with you. As for your connection with the man who owns this house…'

A trace of colour left her smooth features. 'What about Trevor?'

'He knew your whereabouts when I contacted him last week and he lied to me. I'm prepared to let that affront slide if you help me.'

'And if I don't?'

'I can easily make life difficult for him if you don't co-operate. Given the state of his finances…' He let his shrug finish his sentence.

What little colour there was left her face. 'He'll fight you. We *both* will.'

'With what? He's nearly bankrupt. And *you* recently liquidated ninety percent of your assets. The reason behind that isn't yet known to me, but it's only a matter of time.'

'How—?'

Reiko stopped and sucked in a desperate breath. It wasn't worth asking how he knew all this about her. The man she'd known five years ago had possessed the same single-minded intensity in his pursuits.

Only then that pursuit had been his unrelenting desire. For *her*. Not her talent.

Looking into his eyes, she knew he meant every word. And if Damion succeeded in finding out *why* she'd liquidated her assets…

Renewed panic clawed at her insides. The feeling of being cornered, of being exposed, threatened to fling her into the familiar dark void.

Fighting to keep her fraying emotions under control, she moved away from him, but Damion Fortier's gaze tracked her, setting her on edge. 'I never thought you'd resort to blackmail to achieve your goals, Damion,' she bit out.

'And I never thought you'd take a lover *three weeks* after leaving my bed. Let's agree to be deeply disappointed in each other, *cherie*, and move on.'

The ice in his tone froze her spine.

'To sweeten the deal, I'll even pay you handsomely. Two million dollars for locating both paintings.'

Her mouth dropped open at the astounding figure.

A mocking smile touched his lips. 'I thought that might get your attention. Listen to your instinct. Take the deal.'

A sense of inevitability settled on her shoulders. Damion was going nowhere. She could fight, or she could take the money. That sort of money could make a huge difference—change the lives of so many. 'I'll do it. For the two million. But I want something else.'

Grey eyes darkened with thinly veiled contempt. 'Of course you do. What?'

'Invite me to your exhibition.'

'Non,' he negated immediately.

Her lips tightened. 'My talents are good enough for tracking paintings but not good enough for your crowd?'

'Precisely,' he parried without blinking.

His insult bounced off her. He wasn't the first to call her character into question and he wouldn't be the last. Reiko liked it that way. With people busy examining the glossy, showy shell of her carefully honed character, they weren't looking underneath to the scars, the pain of loss and the constant fear that lurked there; they couldn't see the empty darkness in her soul that she battled every waking moment to hide.

She needed the camouflage just as she needed every wit to keep Damion Fortier from finding out just how damaged she'd become.

'I've been out of circulation for a while. If you want me to find your paintings quickly, don't deny me this lead.'

The lead would also give her the chance to find the final Japanese jade statue she'd been attempting to retrieve. Her client's last desperate call rang in her ears—one she hadn't been able to ignore. The digging Reiko had done this past week had pointed her in the direction of a prominent French politician who'd be attending Damion's exclusive exhibition.

When Damion's face remained impassive, she changed tactic. 'Your guest list reads like something out of an art collector's fantasy. I don't think I'll ever get another chance to mingle with people so influential in art or come within a whisper of the famous St Valoire *Ingénue* collection.'

'Your presence anywhere near my exhibition is not something I'd term a fantasy. In fact I'd call it more of a nightmare.'

Despite knowing he wouldn't believe her, she said, 'I'm not a thief, Baron.'

'All evidence points otherwise.'

'I'm an art connoisseur, like you. Just because we took different paths in our pursuit of art doesn't make us any different from each other.'

His haughty expression added insult to injury. 'I highly doubt we're anything alike. You deal *underneath* the black market—'

'I retrieve art no one else can and return it to where it belongs. Isn't that why you're here?'

One silky eyebrow shot up. 'So you're the Robin Hood of the art world?'

She grimaced. 'Green tights aren't my style. Besides, I don't really like labels. Invite me to your exhibition. Who knows? Your squeaky-clean patrons might rub off on me and I'll transform into a model citizen *and* find your precious paintings.'

His eyes narrowed.

Reiko held her breath, fought the urge to speak. Sometimes silence was a better weapon.

'You can work on your transformation in your own time. First you'll agree to use your every resource to find the paintings.'

The gravity and raw need behind his words caught her attention. Glancing at him, she saw something in his face she couldn't give a name to—although she *felt* his near-hypnotic eyes pin her to the spot. In that moment she was almost ready to forget everything she knew about this man and believe the paintings meant something significant to him.

Almost…if she didn't know for a fact that Damion Fortier was a heartless bastard. He'd said it himself—anything that didn't earn him cold hard cash was *sentimental and messy*.

His bloodline might be pure but the man was anything but. In the past five years, the broken hearts he'd left scattered around Europe alone—publicly denied in return for jaw-droppingly extravagant parting gifts but privately mourned—put his status as heartless in direct conflict with his family's sanctimonious image.

As for his year-long affair with Isadora Baptiste…

'Why do you want the paintings so badly?' she asked.

For several minutes she thought he wouldn't answer. A very real emotion that looked oddly like pain settled in his eyes. Her breath caught. Pain was a familiar emotion to her, along with guilt, and panic-inducing demons that haunted her nights. Suddenly the need to know clawed at her, and her heart was thundering wildly as she waited for his answer.

'Why, Damion?'

'I want…I *need* to have them back. My grandfather is dying. The doctors have given him less than two months to live. I have to find the paintings for him.'

CHAPTER TWO

DESPITE THE INDIRECT devastation Sylvain Fortier had caused her, the raw pain behind Damion's words made her insides clench.

Swallowing the lump in her throat, she fought the sudden automatic need to offer comfort, but the words spilled out anyway. 'I'm sorry for…' She stopped. What could she say in such a circumstance?

When she'd been contacted to broker the sale four years ago, she'd known immediately what the *Femme* paintings meant to Damion's grandfather. Her grandfather had told her the history behind them. At the time her first instinct had been to refuse the commission. But she'd convinced herself she'd moved on from Damion's betrayal—that it was merely another business deal. Now, looking into Damion's darkened eyes, she wondered if she'd inadvertently set herself up for this meeting, and for his displeasure when he found out just what she'd done with his paintings.

'Damion, I need to—'

Reiko heard footsteps at the door and her heart sank. A second later, Trevor walked in.

'Sweetheart, what's going on? I thought I heard the guests leave—' Catching sight of Damion, he froze inside the doorway. 'What are you doing here, Fortier?' he demanded, his hands leaving his dressing-gown pockets to clench at his sides.

Damion's set jaw tightened. 'My business is with her, Ashton, not you. And I'd think carefully before lying to me again in future.'

'You should've fetched me the moment he got here, Reiko. After what he did—'

'I didn't want to worry you,' she rushed to interrupt before he could finish. He was acting out of concern for her. His guardian role was one he refused to relinquish despite her insistence that at twenty-seven she was old enough to take care of herself. What she'd been through made it difficult for him to let go.

She placed a hand on his sleeve. Damion Fortier's exquisitely sculpted features tightened as he followed the action.

'My business with Reiko is private. You're interrupting.'

The two men squared off, hostility bristling between them.

With a sigh, she took her guardian's arm. 'It's okay, Trevor. I'll be up shortly.'

Desperate that he didn't reveal anything to Damion, she walked him out of the room and into the hallway. As she mounted the first of the worn carpeted stairs, she saw Damion snatch his phone from his pocket.

She tried to keep her panic down. 'Is it worth me asking who you're calling? Your dungeon-keeper, perhaps? Are you sending for your personal guillotine to finish us off?'

'I was about to arrange to have a list of my guests sent to you, but my guillotine can be arranged if that is how you prefer to conclude our business?' Dark brows winged in a mocking query.

Damion saw relief race over Reiko's face before she concealed it.

The swiftness with which she regained her composure surprised him. The Reiko he'd known had worn her feelings on her sleeve. She'd been open, carefree and sexy as hell with it—

Correction...the Reiko he'd thought he'd known...

His jaw tightened as his gaze swung between the pair in front of him. He noted the familiarity between them, the ease with which they spoke, and the whole tableau filled him with distaste. It was obvious Ashton was her latest lover.

An annoying twinge surfaced inside Damion, tightening even further when Reiko murmured a response to Ashton as he leaned his body even closer to hers.

Damion had never craved attention, never sought it for the purpose of spotlighting himself—even though his life seemed to fascinate the tabloid press and the endlessly vacuous social media. But in that moment Damion admitted he didn't like being ignored. In fact he hated it. He wanted to growl, to shout and draw Reiko Kagawa's attention from the older man. Instead he gritted his teeth and watched as they mounted the stairs and disappeared into the upper hallway, not once looking back.

Swallowing the distinct taste of displeasure that coated his mouth, Damion shoved his hand through his hair. He was seriously considering storming up the stairs when Reiko reappeared alone. The upper-hallway light cast her silhouette in soft relief. Through the material of her dress, Damion traced her shapely legs to where they met at that triangular gap that had once so fascinated him.

Heat slammed into his chest as he recalled how he'd been able to slip his fingers inside her without the smallest need to part her thighs.

Lost momentarily in the past, he let his gaze drift upward, over her curvy hips to the small indentation of her waist where she'd planted her hands. His hands could encompass that small waist. Easily. She'd always melted into his arms when he'd done just that.

'So what now?' she asked.

'Come down here,' he instructed hoarsely.

Catching and killing his wayward thoughts, he shoved his hands into his pockets. She was midway down the steps when he noticed she wasn't wearing shoes. Dainty feet with nails painted a soft peach clashed with the heavy make-up and scarlet lips.

He frowned. 'Are you and Ashton lovers?' he asked, before the question was fully formed in his mind.

Surprise flared in her eyes. A charge of heated energy arced between them. That familiar twinge struck deep, and for the life of him he couldn't dismiss it.

'I fail to see what business that is of yours.'

'I wouldn't want him causing problems with your pursuit of the paintings.'

'He won't be a problem.'

'*Bien.* Give me your phone number.'

'Why?'

'So I can text you the list of names attending my exhibition. Be ready to leave for Paris when I return in the morning.'

'You're not afraid I'll vanish once you leave?' she mocked.

'No. Because you've revealed another weakness.'

Her eyes, a unique hazel that was more brown than green, remained unreadable despite the rapid pulse beating at the base of her slender throat.

'By all means, enlighten me.'

'Aside from the money, you obviously care about Ashton. I can only imagine what you'll do to prevent him from being carted off to jail once I arrange for his debts to be called in.'

A spark very much like anger heated her cheeks. 'Careful, now. That renowned Fortier halo is looking a tad besmirched.'

Damion laughed. The realisation that he was actually enjoying besting Reiko eased the intense frustration of the past few weeks.

'You fight dirty. I fight dirtier. Phone number?'

Tersely, she recited it. He entered it into his phone and pressed 'send'. 'The quicker you strike my guests off your list, the quicker you can move on to find out who has the paintings. You've gained yourself an invitation to my exhibition, but if you have even the faintest urge to pull anything underhand, squash it.'

'Scouts' honour.' She raised two slender fingers.

The folds of her billowing sleeves fell back and Damion caught the faintest glimpse of puckered flesh before she sucked in a breath and tucked her arm against her side. Whirling, she retreated into the shadowed hallway.

Puzzled by her behaviour, he followed. 'Reiko—'

'I didn't get the chance to tell you before Trevor come downstairs.'

'Tell me what?'

'I'll only need to find the *Femme sur Plage.*'

Ice clutched the back of his neck and he forced himself to speak. 'Why?'

'Because I already know where the *Femme en Mer* is.'

'Where is it?'

'In a storage vault in London.'

'Who owns it?'

'I do.'

CHAPTER THREE

THE DREAMS CAME AGAIN… She was laughing as she pulled her father's resistant hand, telling him he had nothing to worry about, that there was space on the crowded train. No, she didn't want to wait for the next train. His hastily concealed concern… his familiar embrace…his strong arms around her.

Then nothing…only the heavy weight of blackness.

And screams—horrible, heart-rending screams—as carnage reigned all round her. Her father's warm hand was clutching hers, then gradually growing cold.

But this time her dreams were interspersed with other images.

Within the chaos Reiko dreamed of dancing with the Baron de St Valoire. And not just any dance. She dreamt of the Argentine frickin' tango.

Reiko woke with her mind filled with vivid images of train wrecks, scarred bodies…and Damion's long, muscular legs tangling with scissor-like precision and skill against her much shorter ones, his hands guiding her with exquisite mastery.

She dreamt of short, shockingly sexy dresses, stratospheric red-soled shoes.

In her dreams the disparity between their heights didn't matter. They fitted perfectly. And when a particular move wasn't possible, her dark-haired, stormy-eyed partner merely lifted her up against his strong, virile body and continued dancing, their heated breaths mingling, his movements getting increasingly faster, headier, sexier—

'What the hell, Reiko?'

Shoving off the offending hot sheets, she went into the bathroom and turned on the shower. She had just over an hour to get ready before Damion returned.

Recalling the incandescent rage that had filled his face after her revelation last night, she swallowed. Weirdly, he'd pulled himself under rigid control after that short display of emotion. He'd told her to concentrate her efforts on finding the *Femme sur Plage*, then he'd left.

After showering, she selected her best power suit. The severe cut of the black jacket and matching trousers coupled with a cream silk dress shirt gave off the no-nonsense vibe she wanted to project, while serving the very useful purpose of covering her up from neck to ankle.

More than anything, she wished she could catch her hair up into a tight bun to cement the outward image she craved, but the scars on her neck made that impossible, so she prayed the suit and make-up would be enough.

After brushing her fringe over the scar that slid down from her temple to her ear, she arranged her hair carefully over her shoulders and slipped her feet into black patent platforms. To complete the look, she secured small diamond studs to her ears.

The heels were a bad idea after the hours she'd spent in another pair yesterday, but there was no way she was putting herself at a disadvantage by wearing flats in Damion Fortier's presence.

She'd pay the price later, with painful stretching techniques and long hours of hydrotherapy, but the idea of going toe to toe with the Baron made it worth it.

Half an hour later, Reiko brushed imaginary lint from her sleeve to avoid Trevor's probing gaze.

'Tell me again why you're doing this, Reiko?' he asked, concern etched into his face.

Reiko contemplated telling him about her bargain with Damion and immediately discarded it. 'Because he's paying me a shedload of money.' She attempted a smile.

He frowned. 'Money has never been your motivation.'

Her smile dimmed. 'Sylvain Fortier is dying, and Damion's

asked me to help find his painting.' The partial truth was better than nothing.

Trevor's lips compressed. 'That's just it, Reiko. After what they did to your grandfather, and to you, they have no right!'

Reiko's heart performed a painful flip but she kept the smile fixed in place. 'That's in the past. I'm over it. Besides, I wasn't joking. He *is* paying me a shedload—some of which can help you—'

He shook his head firmly. 'I can take care of my own financial mess.'

'You took care of me when I needed you. Now it's my turn.'

The lines of worry faded but didn't disappear. 'Did you sleep last night?'

She shrugged. 'A little. Don't worry about me, Trevor. That's an order.'

He laughed, his worry abating to reveal the vibrant fifty-five-year-old man he was, despite his greying hair. Whatever answer he intended to give was curtailed by the sound of a throaty engine in the morning air.

Reiko's heartbeat escalated as she watched the black sports car roar its way down the long lane.

Damion didn't stop in the front drive like any other visitor. He kept coming, his ease behind the powerful car evident in the way his wrist rested on the steering wheel.

His gaze locked on hers, he drove forward until the hood of his car was directly in front of the conservatory. Even with a thick layer of glass between them, Reiko felt the force of his presence, the sheer magnetism of the man, like a crackle of electricity in the air.

Still trapping her with his gaze, he killed the engine and stepped from the car. He'd always had the ability to hold her captive like this, so her every sense was heightened, quaking with awareness.

This morning he'd discarded the designer suit in favour of designer casuals. Dark brown chinos encased his slim hips and ended precisely atop his high-gloss black boots. A slate-grey cashmere jumper worn over a sky-blue shirt did incredibly wonderful things to his eyes.

Watching him mount the shallow steps, she recalled with way too much clarity how his long legs had felt wrapped around her five years ago—and last night in her dreams.

Reeling herself in, she pulled on her cuffs. 'Good morning. I trust today finds you in a less homicidal mood?'

'To see you didn't make a run for it in the middle of night is a good start, *certainement*.'

'You need to have more faith, Baron.'

'I prefer to rely on performance-backed talent.'

'Then it's a good thing I have that in abundance.'

His gaze flicked over her suit. 'Why are you dressed like that?'

'Like what?'

'We're visiting a dusty vault, not attending a state funeral.'

Her belly tightened at his probing look and she forced a careless shrug. 'This is England, Damion. The weather turns at the drop of a hat and I hate being cold.'

She turned with relief as Simpson walked in with her small suitcase. She went to take it but Damion beat her to it. His fingers brushed over hers, making her heightened senses shriek in hysterical warning. But he seemed totally oblivious as he thumbed the electronic key and stowed the case in the boot.

He glanced at the disappearing Simpson and frowned.

'What?' she asked.

'Is this all you're taking with you?'

'Yep, I have a PhD in travelling light.'

His upper lip curled ever so slightly, making Reiko's hackles rise in response. 'I suspect you'd need to, in your profession.'

She felt her smile slip and struggled to keep control. 'If you don't mind, I'd prefer the insults to start *after* I've digested my breakfast. Now, can I have a minute to say goodbye?'

His eyes cooled as they flicked to Trevor. 'Make it quick. I don't have all day.'

She went to Trevor and brushed her lips over his bearded cheek. 'I know you want to clobber him, but try and rise above it, okay?'

Trevor's lips twisted. 'I want to do more than clobber him. But I have to trust you know what you're doing.'

She smiled, despite knowing Trevor would be no match for Damion. The whipcord strength in the Frenchman's broad shoulders and that aura of power that radiated off him meant Damion Fortier need never lift a finger in a show of force.

Straightening, she stepped outside and encountered a stony-faced Damion. A dangerous edge of something she couldn't quite name vibrated off him as he held the passenger door open. The hard slam of the car door rattled her teeth, but she kept the smile on her face for Trevor's sake.

The moment Damion slid in beside her, Reiko found breathing difficult. The already cramped space diminished even further, the mixture of his scent and the smell of the soft black leather of the luxury car made the air intoxicating in the extreme.

Her trembling fingers had barely secured her seatbelt before he was accelerating down the lane.

'You do realise you're not coming back here until after I have my painting?'

She frowned. 'Yes.'

His gaze left the road for a second. 'The size of your case seems to indicate otherwise. If you have any thoughts of returning here any time soon, kill them now.'

'Our agreement still stands. I packed a small case because I didn't want Trevor to worry. Whatever else I need I can get later.'

His lips tightened. 'Does he know of our past?'

'What past?' she taunted and watched his nostrils flare in irritation.

'Is he your only lover or do you have one of those *progressive* relationships?'

'Our relationship is based on truth and trust. More than I can say for whatever it was you and I had.' She sucked in a sustaining breath and wished she hadn't. Damion's scent filled every pore of her being, invading her skin as he'd invaded her dreams last night. 'And, for the record, my relationship with Trevor is none of your business.'

As for *other* relationships…the very thought made her snort bitterly.

Stormy grey eyes sliced into her. 'You find me amusing?' he rasped, his tone chilly.

'Amusing? No. Inappropriate? Definitely. Who I sleep with has nothing to do with this commission. So, before one of us blows our top, I suggest we change the subject.'

His hands clenched over the wheel, his hooded gaze on a red light. As if he'd willed it, it turned green.

Damion's foot slammed on the accelerator, sending the car surging forward.

'I agree. This isn't a subject I find palatable. Why did you buy the *Femme en Mer*?'

Reiko's heart lurched. 'Because it was a good investment and I had the resources to buy it at the time.'

Damion glanced at her before smoothly joining the motorway. 'Was that the only reason?'

She licked her lips, nerves eating at her. 'What other reason would there have been?

His eyes narrowed. 'Foolish sentiment, perhaps?'

'Sentimental? Over *you*?' She tried to inject as much cynicism into her voice as possible.

'I know our time together meant something to you. You wouldn't have been so riled up last night if it hadn't.'

'Wow—conceited much?' Reiko didn't know why she was goading him. But then she'd never been one to leave well enough alone. 'FYI, I got over you pretty quickly.'

His fingers gripped the steering wheel until the knuckles showed white. '*Oui*, I remember,' he clipped out. Minutes ticked by. 'So who was he?'

Reiko felt the familiar wash of shame and looked out of the window. She had no intention of revealing the truth of what had happened in the weeks after Damion had left. It wasn't a time she was proud of, and she planned on keeping it buried along with all her other secrets.

'No one you know. If you really want to know my reason for buying the painting, my grandfather once told me the story behind it. I was intrigued. But I'm willing to set my *sentiment* aside for a healthy return.'

Damion changed lanes again, swerving into the fast lane to pass a slower car. Beneath his trousers, his powerful thigh muscles bunched, the way they had in her dream. And just like in her dream, heat pooled in Reiko's belly and started to rise. Staunchly, she pulled her eyes away and focused on the traffic.

'What exactly *do* you know about the painting?'

There was nothing but curiosity in his tone, but apprehension raced over her skin nonetheless.

'Our grandfathers met your grandmother at the same time. Sylvain Fortier got the girl and the chance to paint her. My grandfather lost out because yours had the most money and power in the love triangle. They remained long-distance friends and business partners until you Fortiers decided your mutual history wasn't worth a damn in the face of your bottom line. Cute story, isn't it? For goodness' sake, slow down! I'd really appreciate arriving in one piece.'

Reiko breathed a sigh of relief as the powerful car eased its frightening pace. Beside her, Damion's brows were clamped in a fierce frown.

Finally he drew to a stop at another set of traffic lights. Stabbing a hand through his hair, he exhaled. '*Cute* is the last term I'd use to describe the story behind the paintings.'

'I was being facetious. Trust me, there's nothing cute about watching someone you care about lose everything. And there's certainly nothing cute about being made a fool of. So unless you want to talk about *that*, I suggest we drop the subject, shall we?'

Stony-faced, Damion shrugged. The rest of the journey was made in silence.

Their escort to the vault in Central London was conducted with reverent haste once the patrons recognised Damion. He stood close as the *Femme en Mer* was removed from the vault and its protective sheets unwrapped.

The painting was of a woman in a barely-there bikini, crashing through frothy waves. Her windswept hair gleamed dark and glossy, the chocolate tresses begging to be touched. Her laughing face, set in profile, was stunning, and drew the eye to her exquisitely detailed features. Around her neck was fastened a thin white scarf that billowed over one shoulder, lending a whisper of innocence to the painting.

But it was her mouth—a sensual mouth so like Damion's that Reiko had to steel herself not to glance at it—that set the woman's beauty apart from the ordinary. The painting was alive. The oils, even after over a half-century, were vibrant and passionate. It was a true masterpiece.

'She was truly stunning, your grandmother,' Reiko murmured, unable to take her eyes off Gabrielle Fortier's image.

'*Oui*, she was.' His tone was firm, but where she'd expected fondness or a little warmth, she heard nothing.

A glance at his face showed the same stony demeanour he'd worn since they stepped out of the car into the quiet London side street.

Curiosity made her continue. 'My grandfather told me she had the whole of the Sorbonne at her feet the two semesters she was there.'

His smile did nothing to alleviate his icy, harsh features. 'I've no doubt that is what happened, because at her feet was exactly where Grandmère preferred her men.'

Her shocked gasp made him raise an eyebrow.

'I've surprised you?'

'I suppose I shouldn't be surprised, but I wasn't expecting… Wow—just…wow.'

'It's the truth. You expect me to mouth platitudes where there are none?'

'Platitudes? Probably not, seeing as you don't *do* sentiment. But isn't it a harsh thing to say about your own grandmother?'

'You know nothing about my life.'

Pain struck sharp. 'Of course I don't. Damion Fortier is a stranger to me. I spent six weeks with a man I knew as Daniel Fortman. But I *do* know about social etiquette and the art of polite conversation. I wouldn't denounce a member of my family the way you do without even blinking. Especially when your family goes to great lengths to project a pristine image.'

'Even angels fall, *mademoiselle*. And I hid my identity simply to avoid this very situation.'

'What situation?' she demanded.

He waved his hand at her. 'This false affront. This pretence that what I did caused any lasting damage. We both know you got over me very quickly, don't we?' he flamed at her.

Heat crept up her neck and engulfed her face. His condemning gaze raked her face but she refused to look away. 'You have no right to look down your nose at me when you lied to me consistently for six weeks. And I don't really care about your reasons for lying. I trusted you enough to give you my body. You didn't return the favour; instead you sent a cheque for a million dollars to salve your conscience. And now you're disappointed I took it? If the money was some sort of test I was expected to pass to be deemed worthy in your eyes, then screw you, Damion. I'm glad I failed—' Reiko bit her lip to stem the flow of words.

The last thing she wanted him to know was how devastated she'd been when she'd received the money after her grandfather's death in place of an explanation. Yes, she could have taken the high road and ripped the cheque to shreds. Instead she'd taken delight in giving away every last cent to her favourite charity.

'…sorry.'

The low, deep word drifted over her, pulling her back from dark recollections. When she glanced at him, he looked slightly shaken—taken aback, even.

'What did you say?'

His features remained taut. 'Perhaps the situation could've been handled differently.'

'No kidding, Sherlock.'

'And for that I'm sorry.'

She heard the words but the condemnation in his eyes didn't dissipate. Slowly it dawned on her what was really bothering Damion. 'It's not about the money, is it?'

'What do you mean?'

'Even though you've apologised, you're still staring at me like I'm pond scum. But it's got nothing to do with the money, has it? It's because you think I sl—'

'I prefer not have this conversation here, Reiko, or indeed at all.' He nodded to the vault attendant who'd been listening raptly to their conversation. The young man hurried forward with the crate.

'That's fine by me.' Reminiscing…*sentiment*…led to nothing but pain. She needed to be as clinical as Damion, see this job through, and make sure the next time she disappeared she stayed hidden for good.

Jaw set in concrete, Damion packed the *Femme en Mer* himself, his gentle but efficient handling of the painting a testament to his years of experience in art-dealing.

The St Valoire auction house dated back to the turn of the nineteenth century, when it had been opened by one of Damion's illustrious forebears, but Damion himself had been the one to open the now world-famous Gallerie Fortier.

In its very short history it had grown to rival Sotheby's and Christie's, specialising in holding prestigious exhibitions ex-

clusively for royalty and heads of state. Only two months ago
the Paris headquarters of Gallerie Fortier had held the first ever
exhibit of twelve stunning diamond-and-emerald-encrusted
Matryoshka nesting dolls, rumoured to have belonged to the
wife of a long-dead tsar. The art world had been abuzz with the
news for weeks, especially as no one had claimed the bounty.

Wrestling to bring things back to neutral ground, she asked,
'Did you ever find out who owned those Matryoshka nesting
dolls?'

Cold eyes looked up from his wrapping of the painting. 'The
rightful owner was tracked down eventually, yes.'

She passed him tape to secure the thick paper around the
painting. Again their fingers touched. Again the surge of heat
made her insides clench. 'Want to share with me who it is?'

'No, I don't. What's your interest anyway? I thought you
were retired?'

She shrugged. 'Semi-retired from art retrieval. I broker from
time to time, and I may have a buyer who's interested in acquiring the whole collection.'

'An anonymous one who prefers to hide in the shadows, no
doubt?'

'Naturally,' she responded drolly.

'Use the right channels, and my people will happily sup-
ply you with the owner's details.' He picked up the crate and
headed towards the exit.

Reiko hurried to catch up. She reached the car just as Damion
stowed the crate in the boot, next to her suitcase.

Slamming the boot, he turned to her. 'Have you ever given
any thought to going straight? Giving up the sordid underworld
in favour of using your talents legitimately?'

'Straight is boring. I like what I do.'

'Serial killers like what they do, too, but they eventually
get caught.'

Unexpected laughter bubbled up from her chest and spilled
out into the mid-morning sunshine. 'You did *not* just compare

me to a serial killer! I thought you French were supposed to be charming?'

The barest hint of a mocking smile lightened his face and his gaze dropped to her feet. 'If the Ferragamos fit…'

Confronted with the less haughty features she'd once been captivated by, Reiko stared. Just then a light wind whipped between them. She felt it tug her fringe away from her face, threatening to expose her scar. Hurriedly she smoothed her hair down and tucked it behind her ear.

But not before she caught Damion's frown. A dart of anxiety stabbed her. What would he think if he saw her scars? Would he be disgusted and pitying? Or would he strive for false indifference as some did when she inadvertently exposed them, as she almost had last night?

The thought made a silent scream rip through her. His lips parted and she *knew* he was going to ask what she was hiding. The urge to curtail the question made her reach out. With her free hand she gripped his biceps. His gaze stayed on her hair for several seconds, then dropped to her hand on his arm.

Despite the sensation crawling over her skin, Reiko kept the smile on her face. 'We have a plane to catch, I believe?'

Grey eyes snapped back to hers. Their gleam told her he knew what she was doing. Thankfully, he didn't push.

The worst of the rush-hour traffic was clearing by the time they rejoined the motorway. Damion handled the sleek sports car with the ease and efficiency of an expert. Slowly Reiko became less tense as the miles flew by.

The signs for Biggin Hill's private airport flashed past before she decided to break the silence.

'So, is it true your exhibition is centred around the *Ingénue* collection?'

'Yes. What else did you hear?'

She shrugged. 'That you're holding the exhibition on February fourteenth.'

'Oui, c'est vrais.'

'Is that like you flipping two fingers at St Valentine?'

He frowned. 'Why would you think that?'

Her choked laughter scraped her throat. 'What else could it be? Surely you don't expect me to think the day holds special meaning for you?'

'Why not?'

'Because you're "about as loveable as an arsenic-coated spike".' When he shot her a furious look, she held up her hand. 'Don't glare at me. I'm just quoting one of your loved-up girl-friends. Or should I say loved-*out*? She wasn't too happy with being an ex-girlfriend, if I recall the article correctly.'

'Don't believe everything you read in your gutter press.'

'*Touché.* But seriously? Valentine's Day?'

His shrug drew her attention to his powerful physique. 'It was the most convenient date and suited all parties. If it adds a little *je ne sais quoi* to the occasion, all the better.'

'Ah…ever the ruthless entrepreneur.' Deep bitterness spiked her heart.

He swung into a hangar marked 'Private' and brought the powerful sports car to a stop at the steps of a large white, gold-trimmed aircraft.

Two men approached, one going directly to unpack the boot. The pilot stood at the bottom of the short flight of stairs, ready to usher them in.

Damion swung his door open, but before he stepped out, he turned to her. 'Don't get me wrong, Reiko. I believe in every-thing February the fourteenth stands for. I just haven't found a woman who shares the same belief with no strings attached.' His gaze dropped to her lips briefly before rising to pin her. 'If and when I do, I will pursue her with the same relentless deter-mination I pursue every other pleasure in my life. And I will let nothing stand in my way until she's mine.'

CHAPTER FOUR

REIKO TRIED TO DISMISS Damion's words. In some ways she could see how the words could be construed as *hot*. She could certainly understand how any *other* woman would find it difficult to think straight after being the object of *that* delivery—especially with that low, gravelly accent thrown in for good measure. After all, hadn't she fallen for the whole package of effortless charisma and sheer animal magnetism?

She desperately tried to stem the incredibly fiery sensation that rose in her belly whenever she remembered his gaze on her lips.

Damion's words would never apply to her. He'd made that glaringly obvious when he'd walked away without a backward glance five years ago.

No, when Damion Fortier chose his mate, he would cast his net in the exclusive pool of privilege and prestige equal to his own, not in the damaged remnants of a brief, meaningless affair.

The aircraft landed and rolled into another hangar at Orly Airport. She jumped from her seat. Damion, who'd been on the phone for the whole flight, hung up and glanced at her. Again the look tugged on her senses, and she hissed in irritation at herself.

She had calls to make, people to contact if she was to establish a solid lead as to the whereabouts of the *Femme sur Plage*. Four years in this shaky economic climate was a long time for a painting to remain in one place for long—especially one as exclusively priceless as the Sylvain Fortier piece. If Damion, with his unlimited funds and excellent contacts, had been unable to locate it, then she'd have her work cut out.

Whom Damion would eventually choose as his Baroness was the last thing she should be thinking of.

Fishing a pen out of her handbag, she quickly scribbled down her address. 'This is where I'll be staying, should you need to contact me. Otherwise I'll see you at the exhibit on Friday evening.'

He glanced at the piece of paper but made no move to take it. '*This* is where you stay when you're in Paris?' The slur in his tone was unmistakable.

'Don't tell me. You wouldn't be caught dead in that neighbourhood?'

'*Oui*, that is right. And neither will you.'

'I always stay there. I like the area's bohemian feel. You should try it some time. Maybe you'll like it.'

'Believe it or not, I've tried it and *liked* it. I lived there during my university days.' He caught her slack-jawed look and smiled. '*Before* it became a drugs and gang hotspot. When was the last time you were there?' he asked.

Recalling the last time she'd visited Paris, she felt a swell of pain rise through her. 'Three years ago.'

A hooded look came over his eyes. 'Were you alone?'

'No.' She'd been with her father. They'd had an amazing time. Going back to where she'd stayed with him would be painful. Of that she had no doubt.

Face the demons...

Damion rose to tower over her. 'Well, you won't be staying there. I won't let you compromise our agreement simply because you want to feel *bohemian*.'

'It's a good thing you're not the boss of me, then, isn't it?' she snapped.

'Look out of the window, Reiko,' he replied simply.

'Why?' Her head whipped to the closest window, her heart hammering. Expecting to find the plane surrounded by police, all she saw was another gleaming sports car and an immigration official ready to inspect their travel documents. Relief made her slightly dizzy. 'Wh…what exactly am I supposed to be looking at?'

'You're not a French citizen, which means you need a special licence or a certificate of origin to bring any form of art into the country. I haven't yet taken ownership of the *Femme en Mer*, so unless I vouch for you, or claim ownership of the painting, the authorities will have to be involved. Now, personally I don't have a problem—'

'Fine! We'll do it your way.' His smug smile made her teeth grind. 'Did I mention that I think you're a cold bastard?'

'Your tone implied it exquisitely.'

'Good, I'm so glad.' Despite her snarky tone, panic began to claw at her insides. She had no doubt Damion meant to keep her close. Which meant he would be within hearing distance should she experience another of her nightmares, or worse. Carefully, she cleared her throat. 'Do you intend to hold me prisoner the whole time I'm here?'

Their pilot came out and lowered the steps to the plane. Damion ushered her out. 'Not at all. You're a free agent. As long as you stay at my apartment, stay within the confines of the law and make every attempt to locate the painting.'

When he placed a hand in the small of her back to propel her forward, Reiko jumped out of reach. Beneath her clothes, her skin tingled. She averted her gaze from Damion's frowning look.

'Let's not keep the nice officer waiting,' she said hurriedly.

His frown remained in place. 'It also goes without saying that I want you on your best behaviour. And, before you use another Scout salute, be warned that I saw your two-finger salute last night instead of the correct three.'

He stood so close she could see the faint shadow of his stubble, smell the heady scent of him. Hurriedly she went down the stairs. 'How would you know? I find it impossible to picture *you* as a Scout.'

'I wasn't, but I had a crush on a Guide once upon a time.'

Stunned, she glanced at him as he shook hands with the official. The sheer magnificence of him made something kick in her chest, catching her breath for a second before releasing it. When Damion's gaze caught hers, she struggled to maintain a neutral expression.

She couldn't lower her guard around him. Even if what had happened five years ago hadn't been enough of a lesson, she only had to think of his affair with Isadora Baptiste to remember she detested everything about his heartless attitude towards relationships.

Like an ice-cold shower, the thought obliterated everything else.

The foundations of her control solidified, she slid into the car beside Damion.

She felt his quizzical gaze on her, but kept hers forward. When he turned the ignition and gripped the gearstick, she deliberately drifted her fingers over the back of his hand. His light intake of breath didn't pierce her re-imposed self-control. Even the tingle in her fingers lingered for a split second before it set her free. For that, Reiko was eternally grateful.

'You don't need to worry. I'll be on my best behaviour.'

'I'm curious as to the sudden change of heart.'

Had his voice grown a little raspier?

'Let's just say I don't want to prolong our association any longer than I have to.'

Damion pondered the change in Reiko as he negotiated the last few streets towards his Parisian apartment in the third *arrondissement*. Something had happened between their disembarking the plane and leaving the airstrip. Something he couldn't put his finger on.

Her body was so still, her expression so remote, Damion wondered if she was in some sort of trance. Only the frequent flickering of her eyelids and furtive glances out of her window indicated she wasn't in a meditative state.

When he pulled up outside his apartment overlooking the Place des Vosges, he glanced at her again. This time she met his gaze. Damion saw a trace of pain in that look and frowned. Had he been too rough with her? A tinge of guilt seeped in to compound his confusion. As feisty as she was, he wasn't unaware of her diminutive stature. His glance slid over her again and his frown deepened. Why had she covered herself up so completely?

The Reiko he'd known had worn skimpy outfits designed to drive him wild with desire. He recalled her perfect, flawless skin, and heat unfurled within him. He'd loved running his hands over her naked body, watching arousal heat her flesh, hearing her words of wonder as he'd taken her...

He stemmed the tide of unwanted memories.

Five years ago he'd let the personal get in the way of business and regretted it.

Whatever Reiko Kagawa was hiding underneath those staid, sexless clothes was no longer his business.

His main focus needed to be on locating the third painting and making sure his grandfather's last days were made as comfortable as possible.

As to what came after that... His jaw tightened. He'd think about that aspect of his duty—finding a wife, making sure his family name continued—when the time was right.

'*Vien*, we're here.' His personal concierge hurried forward and opened Reiko's door. Damion handed over the contents of the boot and turned to her. 'It's lunchtime. I've booked a restaurant close by. Are you okay to walk?'

He caught her look of panic-tinged suspicion before she quickly doused it.

'Of course I am. Why shouldn't I be?' she challenged, her eyes fiery.

He indicated the cobblestoned pavement reminiscent of this part of Paris. 'Those heels look hazardous—'

'They're fine.'

He'd clearly touched a nerve, but Damion didn't know why. 'Let's go.'

The scent of her flowery perfume caught his nostrils as she fell into step beside him. He slowed his pace to match hers, and in the spring sunshine watched the way the light bounced over her long, dark locks.

He felt another puzzle tease at his brain. Her suit, make-up and shoes all shrieked a power statement that her free-flowing hair immediately defused.

Or was that her trick? Recalling the way she'd touched him last night and this morning, Damion felt his gut tighten. The contact had been in no way sensual, and certainly not what he was used to from women, but it had captured his attention. So much so he hadn't been able to dismiss it from his mind.

A *grande dame* tottered past with several dogs on a leash. Reiko didn't seem to notice her. He grabbed her arm to steer her clear of the menagerie and felt the fragile bones of her elbow beneath his touch. He waited for her to make a comment and glanced at her when she didn't.

'What?' she enquired.

He nodded to the old lady. 'You once mentioned how cute you thought that whole *grande dame* with dogs thing. So very French.'

Her mouth dropped open. She looked after the old woman and her dogs, then back at him. 'You remember?'

He remembered a great deal about their six weeks in Tokyo; he had spent far too much time last night thinking about it. Was spending too much time thinking about it now. What the hell was wrong with him?

Everything Reiko had said to him at the vault had been true. He *had* sent her the money to salve his conscience after he'd learnt of her grandfather's death. But deep down he'd hoped she wouldn't take it—that she'd call or come and find him and rip the cheque to shreds in his presence.

When she hadn't, he'd returned to Tokyo, foolishly believing he'd find her, apologise and resume what they'd started. How wrong he'd been.

Ruthlessly, he pushed the images in his brain away. '*Oui*, I remember.' Bitterness slashed through him, mingling with an arousal he refused to acknowledge. Looking away, he glimpsed the discreet entrance to the restaurant. 'We're here.'

He went to take her elbow again, but she pulled away from him under the pretext of greeting the *maître d'*.

Damion suppressed a grim smile. It seemed this new Reiko had developed a penchant for touching at will, but curiously she didn't like the favour returned. He tucked that little morsel to the back of his mind.

'You didn't finish telling me about the exhibition.' When he hesitated, Reiko shrugged. 'I'm going to find out eventually.' She sipped her water, gripping the glass firmly to hide her trembling.

Damion's revelation outside the restaurant had shaken her. So Damion remembered one tiny comment she'd made during their time together? Big deal. It made no sense for her emotions to skitter out of control because of it.

'The *Ingénue* is a collection of firsts—first poems, first paintings, first sculptures. Even the first *haute couture* gown created by Michel Zoltan.'

She was reluctantly impressed. 'Wow, how did you manage that?' The temperamental and very reclusive designer had created the most perfect wedding gown for the last European royal bride, and then promptly declared it to be his last-ever creation.

He shot her a droll look. 'I could tell you, but I'd have to kill you. And all that blood on this perfect parquet floor...'

'Ha-ha—very funny.'

One side of his mouth lifted in a half-smile as he beckoned the hovering *sommelier*. Once Damion had inspected the chilled bottle and the Chablis was poured, she chose her entrée and main and handed the menu to the waiter.

'These works were done before the influence of the outside world—before the artists' innocence was stolen, as it were. The world has never seen an exhibition like this. Most artists believe their first works aren't worthy of publicising.'

'I don't think it's so much that as an unwillingness to bare their souls to the public—especially in the presence of other artists. Artists have very fragile egos.'

'With the right incentive, even fragile egos are malleable.'

Her fingers tightened around the glass. 'Does that translate as everyone can be bought?'

'In my experience, *oui*,' he responded without an ounce of regret, his cold gaze locked on hers.

She carefully swallowed. 'What a jaded life you've led.'

'As opposed to *your* unsullied existence in an ivory tower? Why do you really want to attend my exhibit? And don't tell me it's because of your love of art.'

Reiko was eternally grateful she'd perfected her poker face long before she could speak, because the grey eyes boring into hers made shivers dance down her spine. 'I told you—to explore whatever lead I can to establish the whereabouts of your painting.'

His eyes narrowed. 'So you won't be blatantly poaching my business?'

She shrugged. 'If you're that bothered about it, we could come to an agreement.'

On cue, haughty distaste filled his eyes. 'I don't do backroom deals.'

'Never say never.'

He was about to respond when the waiter brought their entrée. Her thinly sliced ham on a bed of apple and celeriac was exquisite. Opposite her, Damion attacked his own lobster salad with a relish that reminded her of his huge appetite. Watching his hands as he deftly forked food into his mouth, Reiko felt familiar heat invade her belly.

She lowered her gaze to her plate, a shaft of pain slicing through her at the fruitlessness of her feelings.

Even if there were the remotest chance of a physical relationship with a member of the opposite sex, the man sitting before her would not be her prime choice. Damion Fortier appreciated beauty and perfection. She'd been stunned five years ago when he'd shown an interest in her. Of course the reason *why* had eventually revealed itself. Like a gullible fool, she'd let him brush aside her initial scepticism, drawn to him with an intensity she'd found impossible to fight.

His every choice of female since he'd walked away from her attested to the fact that *she* had been a fluke—a step outside his normal circle, which he'd always intended to return to.

No, Damion would never be given the chance to see her physical scars or glimpse the emotional wasteland that had ravaged her soul.

'Is this how you're hoping to convince me to trust you?' His question broke through her agonising thoughts.

'What?'

'You asked me to trust you but your intentions in attending my exhibition put that theory to the test.'

'Finding your painting is my priority. Everything else is secondary. I give you my word.'

He stared at her for an interminable minute. Then he nodded. *'Bien.'* He extended his hand. 'Shall we shake on it?'

Reiko swallowed and stared at the large masculine hand in front of her. When she glanced back at him, the look in his eyes shifted, and a gleam that made her hackles rise passed through the grey depths before the veneer of civility slid back into place.

'I've already promised to be on my best behaviour, Baron.'

'But a handshake is much more…professional than Scouts' honour, *n'est ce pas*?'

His firm reasoning didn't ease her anxiety. Inhaling, she set her fork down and tentatively placed her hand in his.

The heat from his touch singed all the way to her toes. When she tried to free herself, he held her for a few seconds longer before releasing her.

After that he turned into the perfect host.

· Reiko eventually dared to relax a little, allowed the tension to ease out of her body.

Until he reached out and brushed back her fringe. Her skin burned at the laser-like focus of his gaze on her face.

'How did you get that scar on your temple?' he rasped.

CHAPTER FIVE

SHE JERKED BACK from his touch. Her crystal glass sloshed water onto the pristine white tablecloth as she set it down unsteadily. 'Excuse me?'

'It's a simple question, Reiko.'

'It's also a very personal question. Hell, for all you know it might even border on the sentimental! Are you sure you want to dip your toe in those treacherous waters?'

Damion's eyes glittered with a determination that made her insides clench.

'I'm willing to take that chance.'

Every bone in her body fought against lifting her hand to check that her temple wasn't exposed, that the thin scar tissue burning with its exposure was covered. Reiko felt her lips tremble and fought for control.

'I'm not. Anyway, how would you like it if I asked *you* an extremely personal question?' she demanded in a voice far shakier than she'd prefer.

'Answer mine and I'll give you a chance to ask yours.'

She froze in stunned surprise. 'Are you serious?'

He nodded. 'When did it happen?' he demanded.

She glanced down and moved her food around her plate. 'Two years ago.'

'How?' he fired back.

She shook her head. 'I've answered your question. Now it's my turn. You weren't around when your grandfather sold the paintings. Where were you?'

The sudden tension in his frame made her breath stall in her chest. His features hardened, his fingers clenching around his wine glass as his gaze pinned her to her chair. When he answered, his voice held an edge that grated on her nerves.

'I was here in Paris for a while. Then I went to Arizona.'

'Arizona. Of course.' Reiko didn't frame it in a question because she already suspected the answer.

Isadora.

Bile rose in her mouth, along with nausea. Appetite lost, she crumpled her napkin and threw it on the table.

He followed suit and settled the bill.

The walk back to his apartment was tense. His shoulders were held in rigid anger. He made no move to take her elbow, for which she was…*glad*. Just before they reached his building, he turned to her, eyes narrowed.

'What did you mean by "of course"?'

She glared back at him. 'I heard the Arizona rumours. You confirmed it.'

'What else did you hear?' he asked, tension escalating until it was a living force field around them.

'Nothing that matters.'

His face grew colder.

When he opened his mouth, she held up her hand. 'Seriously, I don't need any more details.'

'I wasn't about to offer any. Merely to suggest that whatever you think you know, keep it to yourself.'

Because he didn't want Isadora Baptiste upset? Despite being close-lipped about the famous designer, everyone knew the truth about their sordid affair.

She shrugged. 'I think we've exchanged enough delightful morsels about ourselves for one day, don't you?' Mounting the shallow steps, Reiko prayed he'd drop the subject.

In silence, he led her into his apartment. She looked around and drew in a stunned breath.

The mezzanine apartment was overwhelmingly beautiful.

Black and white tiles reminiscent of the floor tiles in Versailles gleamed with a high polish. Tall, light-emitting windows overlooked the winding Seine and the Place des Vosges, and in the distance the iconic Tour Eiffel rose proudly.

There wasn't a single curtain or drape in sight, which, for a man who valued his privacy as much as Damion did, surprised her. Beyond the slightly opened window, sounds emitted from the street, bringing with them a soft breeze that flowed into a sunken living room decorated with deep blue wide sofas, boldly designed coffee tables and a state-of-the-art entertainment centre.

And, of course, being the home of a French art connoisseur, it had sculptures, paintings and tasteful works of art displayed in a wealthy tapestry that made the art-lover in her want to fall to her knees in adoration.

Damion dropped his keys onto a nearby table, startling her from her avid inspection of the breathtaking space.

She whirled away from a miniature marble depiction of Psyche and Cupid locked in an embrace set underneath a low light and slammed straight into the hard-packed body of Damion Fortier. She stumbled. Pain ripped through her pelvis. Sucking in a breath, she tried to free herself from the arms that banded her.

But her struggles only made her more aware of the heat and sensual energy emanating from his body.

All the time and effort she'd expended on wrestling back control started to crumble. Reiko wanted to weep.

He frowned. 'Are you all right?'

'Yes. Let me go!'

After a few tense moments, he set her free. 'Watch out for the floors. They can be slippery.'

'Noted. Would you mind showing me where my things are? I need my laptop.'

Gaze hooded, he nodded. After a quick tour of the apartment, he led her down a hallway decorated in the same tasteful manner as the rest of the apartment.

Her suite was immense, blending ancient—a solid antique divan that wouldn't have been remiss in Madame de Pompadour's bedchamber—with twenty-first-century modern comfort—an ergonomic chair and a desk that housed her laptop, with several outlets for her smartphone and electronic accessories.

In the *en suite* living room a curved sofa faced a large-screened TV and entertainment centre, as well as a miniature drinks cabinet. Beneath her feet, Aubusson rugs led to the bathroom, and on two sides of the room, the floor-to-ceiling windows were repeated, giving stunning views over the water. Again without a single privacy-shielding drape or shutter in sight.

She turned to find Damion once again close. Too close. She caught his scent and breathed it in before she could stop herself.

'You have something against drapes?'

He indicated the remote. 'These two buttons regulate the privacy settings on the windows.'

'Oh, good. For a minute there I wondered whether you'd become a shameless exhibitionist.'

She took the control and aimed it at the window. The first button frosted the windows completely, turning them an opaque white that cut off the view. The second button shielded the window halfway, so only the skyline above the river was visible. She left it at that setting and faced Damion, who stared back at her with a probing scrutiny that set her teeth on edge.

'I need to get on with my work, so if you'll excuse me…?'

He pointed to a high-tech console beside the desk. 'If you need anything, press the first buzzer. Fabrice, my butler, will respond. I'm leaving for the gallery now. I don't expect to be back until later this evening. *Bonsoir*, Reiko.'

He left with a soft click of the door. Reiko stood in the middle of the room, feeling deflated and unsure of herself.

She hated the feeling.

Clutching the remote, she gazed at the stunning beauty of her surroundings, at the pieces of art—each more exquisite and priceless than the last. But it was the bed that held her attention. Despite its jaw-dropping beauty, she knew it wouldn't provide a reprieve from the nightmares that had haunted her since the crash. Really, she'd be better off sleeping on the couch, away from main door that led to the rest of the apartment, just in case…

Mind made up, she set to work.

When Fabrice knocked on the door several hours later, Reiko was on the phone to Japan. She listened patiently as the older woman, a member of the same support group Reiko belonged to, sobbed. Gently putting her on hold, she answered the door and said, yes, she'd have a tray brought to her room.

Reiko refused to acknowledge that the need to stay in her room had anything to do with hiding from Damion's prying eyes.

She was here to work.

Turning from the door, she winced as pain shot through her abdomen.

Her fingers drifted to her stomach, where beneath her suit further evidence of her trauma marred her flesh in a permanent, vivid reminder of what she'd been through.

Suddenly her reassurances to the older woman sounded hollow. How could she offer someone else hope when she herself had lost everything—even the ability to be a real woman?

'What are your plans for today?' Damion asked, pulling back his cuff to glance at his watch.

Reiko's eyes darted to him and looked away again. The sunlight caught the tip of her eyelash as it swept down to hide her eyes.

He stared, unsure what was different about her this morning.

Granted, her attire was different. She'd exchanged the power suit for a softer look—jeans, long-sleeved striped top teamed with a stylish jacket, and that signature flowing mane. The constant tension he sensed in her was still there but, looking closer, he saw her skin was flushed—the way he remembered it after she'd had a warm shower…or after making love.

He shifted, and frowned at the direction of his thoughts. He sipped his espresso, hoping the kick would obliterate the heat rising in his groin. She extended her slim hand to lift her cup, her brown-green eyes darting to him once again before flitting away to stare at the morning activity on the river.

'I thought I'd go to the Louvre. I never pass up the chance when I'm in Paris.'

'Whatever you do, don't attempt to whisk away the *Mona Lisa*.'

Her eyes rolled. 'She's not my type. If I had a choice, I'd go for Julien's *Gladiateur*.'

Her answer hit him like a cold bucket of water in his face. 'If that's the type of man you prefer, why are you with Ashton?'

Her tension increased. 'I see we're back to personal territory. Are you willing to play *quid pro quo* again? Only you went all Arctic on me yesterday when swapping questions was *your* idea.'

'Do you treat everything in life like a game? Does it make it easier for you to treat your body like a commodity if it's all a game to you?'

Lushly glossed lips firmed. 'Is that your unsubtle way of asking me if I sleep around?'

Damion's chest tightened. 'Do you?'

'Why are you so hung up on my sex life?' she fired back.

'Why are you wasting your sex life on an old man?'

'Is it the thought of me with any man that bothers you, or just the thought of Trevor and I?'

His jaw clenched. Hard. He refused to examine why the subject bothered him so much. After what he'd witnessed five years ago, it shouldn't. And yet it did.

After several seconds, she sighed. 'Would you believe me if I told you there was nothing sexual between us?'

The blast of relief surprised him before he dismissed it. 'The way you touch him, the closeness between you two, extends beyond mere—'

Her fingers arrived on the back of his hand, the soft caress fleeting and yet so forceful it dried up his words. Damion stared at his tingling skin, unable to stop the arousal rising through him. He hadn't been able to stop it rising since he'd seen her again two nights ago.

'You've just proved my point.' He heard his hardened tone and acknowledged that having his point proved this time was far less palatable than he wished. 'This is all a game to you. But it's a very dangerous game you're playing, Reiko.'

Fabrice approached with a fresh platter of croissants. Reiko greeted him with a wide smile. Before Damion's eyes, his normally staid manservant melted. When her hand shot out and touched Fabrice's elbow in thanks, Damion's insides clenched hard.

'I touch everyone, in case you haven't noticed,' she said once Fabrice left.

'Yes, I've noticed. Obviously Ashton isn't territorial.'

Her eyes connected with his. 'Unlike you?'

'I'm extremely possessive. I don't react kindly when something of mine is poached.'

'Save the caveman stuff for your future wife, Damion.' She busied herself with buttering a croissant—one she seemed to have no interest in eating. 'Didn't I read somewhere you were scouring Europe for the perfect baroness?'

Ice clamped the back of his neck and slithered down his spine. 'I intend to marry sooner rather than later, yes.'

Her hands stilled for a moment, then she continued buttering.

'Then shouldn't you be concentrating on that and staying out of my private life?'

Damion felt a stab of disquiet as the weight of responsibility pressed down harder on his shoulders. Once his grandfather was gone, he would become the sole remaining Fortier. He'd known for a while that he needed to marry and advance his family line. But the thought of marriage and the mind games that inevitably came with it left a coating of distaste in his mouth.

One obsessive relationship was enough for any child to endure growing up. The two Damion had endured had scarred him in a way that had made him wonder at an early age if he was appropriately wired to sustain another relationship. That theory had been tested and found severely lacking with his misjudgement of Reiko and his abject failure with Isadora.

The thought of making the wrong choice again left a knot of anxiety in his chest. One that only blackened his mood.

Tossing back the last of his espresso, he set the cup down. Below him, Parisians went about their morning business. He had back-to-back meetings extending well into the day. Yet he lingered.

'I have more pressing things to attend to now. But when the time comes, there will be no hasty decisions. My mate will be chosen very carefully, and she'll be grateful for the care I took to select her.'

He watched her mouth drop open, a look of incredulity wash over her face.

'Wow, did you just hear yourself? You're seriously amped up on your own power juice, aren't you? I guess five hundred years of lording it over humanity would do that to you, huh? But you don't know what's around the corner.' A look—part pain, part bitterness—crossed her face, shadowing her sunlit features. 'One minute you're walking around thinking you own the world, the next it can all be taken from you.'

'Is that what happened to you?' His gaze drifted to the left side of her face, where the heavy fringe was once again in place. Damion had a meeting in twenty minutes. He needed to leave. 'Tell me about it.'

Her fingers shredded the croissant. When her gaze finally lifted to his, her eyes were devoid of emotion. 'Stop prying into my life, Damion.' She stood, and Damion was reminded how tiny she was without her heels. 'I don't want to be stuck in the queue outside the Louvre for hours. I need to spend at least one hour with the *Odalisque*.'

'Why?'

'Because anything less than an hour with her is an insult. See you later.' She wiggled her fingers in a careless wave, but he sensed a brittle fragility in her that struck an unsettling chord within him.

He cast another impatient glance at his watch. 'Dinner will be ready by seven. Make sure you're back by then.'

She looked ready to protest. He deliberately turned away to pick up his suitcase. By the time he straightened, she was leaving, her oversized handbag banging against her hip. He watched her walking away, unable to tear his gaze from the lustrous mane swinging down her back to touch her pert little backside. With a frown he noticed her jeans were far too tight, moulding her hips in a way a lover's hand would.

Another stab of white heat pierced his groin. He swore low and hard.

Reiko moved from room to room, determined to use the richness around her to obliterate thoughts of Damion.

But it seemed even the paintings and sculptures in the Louvre were conspiring against her. The strong, perfectly sculpted body of *Oedipus* brought to mind Damion's hard-packed body when she'd slammed into him yesterday. The eroticism of *David and Bathsheba* reminded her of last night's twisted erotic dreams, heavily featuring Damion Fortier.

By the time she entered the Richelieu Wing, frustration lurked a tiny scream away. Maintaining a neutral expression for Philippe, the curator's personal assistant, whom she'd found waiting with a VIP pass when she'd arrived at the museum, was intensely difficult.

She refused to let the fact that Damion had arranged this for her touch her in any way. The only reason she could think of was that he *really* wanted her back by seven.

'Do you wish to return to Goya's *Countess*, or perhaps the *Odalisque*?' Philippe asked. 'The room containing the *Odalisque* has been cleared for your personal viewing.'

'*What?* Why?'

Philippe smiled. 'I believe the curator was told it is your favourite room in the Louvre.'

'It is…but…he can't just clear it!'

'We don't do it often. Only for special guests of Baron de St Valoire.'

'And how many "guests" have there been?' The words tripped out of her mouth before she could stop it. 'Oh, please—ignore me. I'm not normally this… Ignore me.' She touched Philippe's sleeve and his perturbed look dissipated.

Reiko followed Philippe back to the Sully Wing, myriad feelings churning through her belly.

Special guests of Baron de St Valoire.

Reiko shoved the emotion she was reluctant to acknowledge as jealousy aside and stood in quiet contemplation, studying the woman who'd been doomed to die but had faced her death with such dignity and courage.

Who cared who else Damion had done this for? It was a rare treat, and she had every intention of enjoying it.

After an eternity, she turned to thank Philippe—only to find herself alone.

With one last look at the haunting painting, she hitched her bag over her shoulder and slowly made her way outside.

Walking along Rue de Rivoli, she stopped at a patisserie and ordered a panini and a *café au lait*.

Weariness tugged at her senses. Nightmares had plagued her again last night—this time in even more vivid detail. She'd awoken on the couch in a sweat, heart pounding, with images of burning bodies in her mind. Luckily she hadn't screamed. For hours she'd been afraid to go back to sleep. When she finally had, she'd dreamt of dancing with Damion—again in exquisite, erotic detail. They'd touched almost everywhere except their lips. Again he hadn't kissed her, but she'd read the intent in his eyes, in his every breath.

The ache in her belly and between her thighs when she'd

woken this morning had taunted her—a cruel reminder of what she could never have pressing down on her until tears had welled in her eyes.

But even her quiet sobs hadn't erased the intense feelings. She'd barely been able to look Damion in the eye at the breakfast table.

She jumped as her phone rang. Frowning at the unfamiliar number, she answered it.

'So—two hours with the *Odalisque*?'

Damion's deep voice felt like a caress against her ear.

Surprise gave way to suspicion. 'Did you arrange the VIP treatment so you could keep tabs on me?'

Silence greeted her accusation. Then, 'I think the words you're looking for are *Thank you, Damion*.'

'Not if you're spying on me, Baron.' Perhaps she was overreacting, but hearing his deep, accented voice so soon after reliving her dreams unsettled her.

'Do I need to?' His voice held an edge to it.

'Of course not.' she muttered.

'*Bien sûr.* I called the curator to find out if you were being looked after. He told me you'd finished your tour and left.' He waited expectantly.

She bit her lip, breathed in deeply. 'I thoroughly enjoyed my visit. Thank you for organising it. But I hope you don't think this grants you a free pass to start prying into my life again.'

'I know enough to satisfy me for now. Don't be late.'

The line went dead.

Reiko stared at the phone, her heart rate suddenly rocketing in a way that made her breath catch. With shaking fingers, she tried to call him back but the number was engaged.

He doesn't know, she reassured herself, but anxiety twisted through her as she made her way back to Damion's apartment three hours later.

Fabrice let her in and informed her Damion was on his way home.

She took a few minutes to run a brush through her hair and fix her lipstick. She came downstairs just as Damion walked through the door.

The sheer magnetism of the man was off the scale. She couldn't take her eyes off him as he walked, lean-hipped and broad-shouldered, towards her. When his eyes raked her from head to toe before returning to capture her gaze, her insides twisted in alarm.

Keep calm, he doesn't know.

But no matter how much she berated herself, her pulse just thundered harder.

'What did you mean earlier on the phone?' she demanded before she could stop herself.

His brow lifted along with an enigmatic smile that set her teeth on edge. '*Bonsoir* to you, too.'

Panic hammered beneath her skin but she refused to let it run free. 'Please answer me.'

Fabrice appeared, took Damion's briefcase and melted back into the hallway. Damion's gaze stayed locked on hers.

Reiko licked her lips. 'Tell me what you meant or I'll walk out of here right now and you'll never find your painting.'

He tensed slightly, then exhaled. 'Put away your claws, kitten. I won't hurt you.'

The unexpected gentleness stopped her breath. She stared at him, dread rising within her at the look in his eyes.

No, he couldn't know. But the hairs on her forearms tingled with acute premonition. With every fibre of her being, she wanted to silence him before he spoke, but there was no way to prevent it.

'Tell me about your accident, Reiko.'

CHAPTER SIX

'How…HOW DID YOU find out?'

'You're not the only one who has access to information, Reiko.'

His tone was soft, careful. Next she'd read pity in his face.

Anger and pain rose through her. 'Why would you do that?'

'I'm an impatient man. I needed to know what had happened to you—especially if it would jeopardise your assignment.'

She come down the last step and glared up at him. 'So you thought you'd go ahead and dig a little deeper just to satisfy your curiosity? Despite my giving you my word that I'd make finding your painting my priority? Wow, what a prince you are.'

'Calm down.' He took her elbow and led her to the dining room, where exquisite silverware was set out on a long, intricately designed red cherrywood table.

She rounded on him. 'Don't tell me to calm down. And do you seriously think I'm going to eat with you when you've just informed me that you've spent the day adding a few more pages to my glorious dossier?'

A hooded look entered his eyes. 'There are no more pages because I don't have the full details of your accident.'

Stunned, she stared at him. 'You don't? But I thought…'

He shrugged. 'I've asked for the investigation to be stopped. I'm hoping *you'll* fill in the blanks.'

The idea of letting him have even the tiniest glimpse of the physical and emotional wreck she'd become sent a bolt of pure panic through her. 'If you expect me to be grateful for that, you're going to be sorely disappointed.' She couldn't stop the snark from spilling over. The truth was she already felt exposed at Damion's continued scrutiny, and she had a horrible feeling that sensation would only worsen the longer she spent in his company.

'Sit down, Reiko.'

An unexpected spark of electricity zinged through her belly at the way he said her name, uttering the Japanese intonation perfectly.

Coming up behind her, he held out her seat. She sat, all the while feeling his gaze on her. He was still staring at her when Fabrice walked in with their first course a minute later.

She picked up her spoon but made no move to touch the chilled cucumber *velouté* served with braised chicken.

'You aren't staying with Ashton because you're involved with him, are you?'

Her smile felt brittle. 'No, he was my father's friend and is a surrogate uncle to me. You made your sordid assumption. I let you run with it.'

His gaze raked over her face, probing deeper. 'What happened to you?'

Exasperated with his relentless digging, she put down her spoon. 'Please leave it alone.' She stood and raked back her chair.

'Where do you think you're going?'

'I've lost my appetite. Enjoy your dinner.'

'Sit down.' His voice held a ring of steel that anyone would have been a fool to dismiss. But she wasn't in the mood for his high-and-mightiness.

'Unless you have thumbscrews at the ready, there's no way I'm not walking out of here.'

'That can be arranged.'

'Oh? Is that growly French manliness supposed to turn me on or frighten me?'

'I'll find out one way or the other. I prefer to get the facts from you.'

She stared down at him. 'Why is it so important to you?'

A look passed through his eyes before his lids descended.

'Let's just say I've learnt the hard way not to ignore warning signs. Eat your food.'

Slowly she sat and picked up her spoon with shaky fingers. She managed to swallow her first mouthful despite the lump in her throat.

'Is that enigmatic statement supposed to make me bare my soul to you?'

'No, it's not.' With a heavy sigh, he set down his spoon. 'Your accident had an impact on you. I'm just trying to understand—'

'I don't need psychoanalysis, Baron. I already have a therapist!' The shock on his face made her laugh—only it came out more like a cracked snort. 'I've done the whole twelve-step programme and collected the badges along the way. And before you state the obvious—no, the therapy *isn't* working.'

His jaw tightened. 'Don't put words in my mouth.'

'Whatever. I don't know why you keep pushing. You can't *fix* me, so save yourself the trouble.'

'What happened to break you?'

'You mean other than being a gullible idiot and not seeing that you'd set out to ruin my grandfather?'

His face darkened, but this time Reiko thought she glimpsed a hint of regret in his eyes.

'That was not my intention. I was in the middle of opening the Tokyo branch of Gallerie Fortier when my grandfather asked me to investigate what was going on with your grandfather. I merely reacted to the facts and figures in front of me. If I'd known he'd take it so badly—'

'Your pity is five years out of its use-by date, Baron.'

'Did you know he owed three times what I agreed to let him repay?'

She hadn't known. Confusion mingled with all the different emotions rampaging through her. 'Is that piece of news supposed to soften me up?'

'It's supposed to tell you that I'm not *always* the heartless bastard you think I am.'

Perhaps it was the soft yet implacable assertion. Or maybe it was the large hand that suddenly gripped hers, threading warm fingers through her cold, numb ones. Or it might have been the weariness digging into her soul, causing fresh tears to gather behind her eyes.

Whatever it was, Reiko did the last thing she'd ever intended to do. Staring into Damion's face, she whispered, 'You want to know what happened to break me? Watching my grandfather suffer came close enough, but being responsible for my father's death…? Yep, that clinched the deal.'

Damion witnessed the soul-shattering pain that crossed her face and felt his chest tighten in response.

A shudder raked through her frame, and her face was almost white from the effort it had taken her to utter the words. He reached over and removed the spoon from her grip, laid it down. He, like her, had lost his appetite.

Deep inside he wondered why he was doing this when he'd been so determined not to get personal. Then he thought of Isadora. He'd foolishly taken everything she'd said at face value, hadn't probed enough until it was too late.

'How were you responsible?' he asked.

Haunted eyes met his. 'Why are you doing this? You're not insensitive enough not to notice that this isn't an easy subject for me, so why do you pursue it?'

His unease increased. 'I don't mean to distress you—'

A harsh laugh broke from her lips. 'You're doing a stellar job, regardless.'

His jaw clenched. 'You're as fragile and brittle as sheet glass. One push in the wrong direction and you'll shatter.'

'Then stop pushing!'

He tightened his grip. 'You said yourself the therapy isn't working. How long do you intend to bury this?'

Angry colour surged into her cheeks. 'Spare me your pop psychology.'

'Don't get snippy.'

'Back off, Fortier. I might look small but I can hurt you. I'm Japanese. Ninja skills are in-built. I can kill you with a single look.'

Despite the fierceness of her tone, he laughed. 'You're only half-Japanese. And I thought ninjas weren't supposed to reveal their true status?'

He saw her relief at the change of subject and gave her a little reprieve.

She shrugged. 'It's only fair to forewarn you. I wouldn't like you to think I've taken unfair advantage.'

Her lips trembled, and his heart clenched again.

Before he could stop himself, he brushed his thumb over her lips. Softness registered, along with an intense need to remind himself of her sweet taste.

Bravo, Damion.

'I mean it, Damion. Don't make me kick your ass.'

Sudden fire flamed through his groin.

'Say my name again,' he instructed, before the thought had fully formed.

Wariness entered her eyes. 'Why?'

'I've always loved the way it sounds on your lips.'

'Damion…'

Fabrice walked into the dining room. Damion cursed under his breath and sat back. The anxious look on Fabrice's face when he saw their barely touched plates immediately abated when Reiko smiled at him.

'It's my fault, Fabrice. I think I'm still digesting the panini I had at lunch.'

Fabrice nodded. 'Would *mademoiselle* like a lighter main course, perhaps?' he suggested.

Reiko shook her head and touched his sleeve.

Everything inside Damion clenched—much tighter than it had this morning. The sensation seemed to knock the breath out of him. With ruthless force, he shoved it aside and focused, to find her accusatory gaze fixed on him.

'No, I'm sorry, Fabrice. I don't think I can eat anything else,' she said.

His butler took the news with annoyingly obsequious grace. *'Pas de quoi, mademoiselle. Et pour vous, Baron?'*

Damion dismissed him with a shake of his head. After Fabrice had left, Damion glanced over and watched her tuck a strand of hair behind her left ear.

She looked up and caught his gaze. 'What?' she asked. 'If you're going to accuse me of ruining your dinner, forget it. You performed that magnificent feat all on your own.'

His teeth hurt from being ground together. 'I wasn't. I've lost my appetite, too.'

'Well, hard-core interrogation has a habit of doing that to you. Here's a tip—next time do it *after* your belly is full of Michelin-star-quality goodness.'

Damion didn't answer. He stared at her, unable to shake the single disturbing thought running through his head.

He *hated* the thought of Reiko touching other people.

Reiko woke up just after midnight in excruciating pain. In her distress after the disastrous dinner with Damion, she'd forgotten to do her exercises. All she'd sought after bidding him a terse goodnight had been escape.

She'd collapsed onto the couch, knowing there was no way she would sleep.

How wrong she'd been. Not only had she slept, she hadn't been haunted by nightmares.

Only unbearable pain.

She gritted her teeth against the pain shooting through her pelvis and struggled to regulate her breathing. In the end she knew she had no choice but to do something about it. Gingerly she struggled into her Lycra unitard and made her way to the sleek state-of-the-art gym Damion had shown her when they'd toured the apartment yesterday. Ignoring the highly sophisticated gym equipment, she grabbed a bottle of water and headed for the far side of the room.

Lowering herself onto the mat in front of a mirrored wall, she took a sip of water and breathed in deeply. The first series of exercises were so painful her skin was covered in sweat by the time they were over. But she knew the next set—the knee thrusts—would be even more painful. The very thought of them made her moan in despair.

'I don't quite know how to interpret a beautiful woman moaning in my gym in the middle of the night. Alone.'

Her head snapped towards the voice. Damion leaned in the doorway, wearing sweat pants and a tight white T-shirt, with tousled just-got-out-of-bed hair. Heat slammed into her chest even as she hastily pulled the grip from her hair so her fringe fell over her face. The high neck and long sleeves of her outfit thankfully covered the parts of her body she needed to be covered.

'You're losing your touch, obviously. This is a one-woman show to which you're *not* invited.' She fervently prayed he'd take the hint and leave.

He didn't. With slow, assured strides, he came forward until he stood directly over her. From her position on the floor, Reiko was treated to the simply magnificent landscape of his body—strong legs, trim waist, ripped ridges on his abdomen that rose and curved into a wide, powerful chest…the bulge in his trousers she tried very hard not to stare at despite the blood rushing faster through her veins.

'What are you doing?' he asked.

'What does it look like? I'm exercising.'

'You're in pain. Why?'

'Go away, Damion.'

'If you wanted to keep what you were doing a secret, you would've stayed in your room.'

She blew out an exasperated breath. 'Trust me, I would have

if I'd known you'd subject me to another interrogation. It's wearing seriously thin, by the way.'

He merely shrugged and waited.

Her gaze slid away from his. 'I have a back and pelvic injury from the accident. I was on my feet for too long today and forgot to stretch before bed.'

'You woke in pain?'

She heard the frown in his tone.

She nodded. 'The pain increases when my body stiffens.'

He dropped smoothly onto his haunches, caught her chin in his hand and turned her gaze to his. 'How can I help?'

'You can go away and leave me alone to get on with it.'

The implacable look in his eyes told him he would be doing no such thing.

She sighed. 'Damion—'

'We've performed this dance before, *ma belle*. Tell me how to help you.'

Sighing, she collapsed back onto the mat. 'I told you, I don't need—'

He leaned over and placed his hands on either side of her hips. Her breath snagged in her chest as he reared over her. Glossy chocolate waves fell over his forehead as his eyes bored determinedly into hers. Damion Fortier was going nowhere—of that she had no doubt.

Her only option was to get this over with as quickly as possible. Having him this close bombarded her with haunting, painful memories.

She sucked in a quick, woefully inadequate breath. 'Hold my feet against your chest and push against my resistance. No matter how much I whine, don't stop. Okay?'

Concern darkened his eyes. 'This whining—will it take the form of tears or screams?'

'Either. Both. If you're squeamish, leave now.'

'I'm not squeamish,' he answered, although a look of unease had settled over his face.

He positioned himself on his knees and glanced at her bare legs. For endless moments he just stared at them.

'Come on, Baron, don't wuss out on me. Unless you can conjure a thermal jet pool for me, this is the only way—so let's get on with it.'

His lips firmed. 'Raise your legs.'

She carefully raised them. With firm, strong hands he grabbed her ankles and settled her feet on his chest.

The initial shock of the contact obliterated the pain in her pelvis for several seconds. Fiery currents travelled up her ankles, shot through her calves to concentrate in a steady pulse of delicious heat between her thighs. Of their own accord her toes flexed against his muscled chest as if they were remembering another time, another place.

His chest lifted in a heavy inhale. 'What now?' he rasped.

'Slowly pull my knees apart as you push towards me.'

Warm hands cupped her knees. Gauging her reaction, he leaned down in a slow, steady forward movement.

Reiko bit her lip as pain surged through her pelvis. She clenched her hands against her side, fighting to keep her breathing steady.

'Are you okay?' His eyes had darkened until they were almost black, and the look of concern in them touched a place inside her she most definitely did not want touched.

Swallowing, she nodded. He kept up the momentum, pushing her knees closer to her chest, coming closer, until she could see the faint stubble grazing his jaw. When her heels touched the back of her thighs, she let out a shuddering breath.

'Back, please. Then repeat,' she said, wishing her voice didn't sound so husky. So...*needy*.

He slowly sat back. They repeated the process. On the third round when she moaned, he swore and stopped.

'No, don't stop. I'm okay.'

'You're obviously not. You're crying—'

'I'm *not* crying!'

'Your eyes are leaking—'

'It's just sweat, for goodness' sake. Do it!'

She groaned as he grasped her ankles and repositioned her feet on his chest. By the time he'd repeated the process, her muscles had started to loosen. With the lessening pain she became even more aware of Damion as he surged over her. His powerful aura surrounded her; his scent dominated her every breath. When he drew closer her gaze fell to the smooth, defined curve of his mouth.

She'd always liked him on top...

Like a flash flood, memories rushed through mind—how it had felt the first time they'd kissed, the feel of his hard, hot body against hers, his thick hair between her fingers, the power of his potent manhood as he'd possessed her that first time in her grandfather's cabin in Tokyo. The sheer bubble of joy she'd lived in for weeks after that...

Right from the start the power of his attraction had held her enthralled. She'd been caught up in the sizzle of sensation from the first time he'd introduced himself as Daniel Fortman, a young man she'd assumed was merely a business acquaintance of her grandfather's.

She'd known before they'd exchanged a single word that he would be dangerous to her. But even by then it had been too late. She'd handed herself over to him heart, body and soul. And he'd ripped her apart.

Her thoughts coalesced into a hard knot in her belly, along with a sadness that made tears prickle in her eyes. Proper tears this time—not the pain-evoked, sweat-mingled tears she'd brazenly explained away moment ago.

She was so focussed on not losing it in front of him that she hardly felt Damion lowering her legs on either side of him, or slowly levering himself over her until he filled her vision.

'Tears this time. Don't deny it,' he rasped hoarsely, his breath washing over her face.

She studiously avoided eye contact, preferring to focus instead on the steady pulse beating at his throat. 'Fine. Yes, I'm crying. Deal with it.'

Through the haze of tears, she watched him lower himself further over her, his forearms trapping her body on either side. Her misery receded, her every sense caught up in the altered purpose of Damion's stance. His head lowered another fraction and her pulse raced faster.

'Do you ever think about us?'

His voice, low, intense, caught her on the raw.

'No, I don't,' she lied. 'Why should I?'

'Because of this.'

His gaze dropped to linger on her mouth, setting off a deep tingling. She was vaguely aware of his fingers toying with strands of her hair, but was too focused on the promise of those lips to concentrate on anything else.

And when that promise was fulfilled, the explosion of joy that stormed through her left her reeling. Hot, firm, his mouth teased hers, brushed against it, drawing out the pleasure in a series of touches that made her move restlessly beneath him.

The tiny mole above her lip, which she considered a flaw but recalled he'd adored, became an erogenous zone as his tongue flitted against it. He teased, tugged at her lips for endless pleasure-stoking moments, before he finally deepened the kiss.

A moan far different from the one she'd uttered minutes ago broke through the heated silence of the gym when his tongue boldly caressed hers. With her arms trapped, she couldn't touch him the way she wanted to, but she was already drowning under the sensations coursing through her, and willingly surrendered that particular pleasure. Instead she stroked his tongue with hers, her teeth nipping the end of it as it plunged deeper into her mouth.

His moan of pleasure fired her up. Molten heat coursed through her body to pool in her belly. Her nerves tingled with an electric spark only this man seemed able to ignite.

She gave up completely when his fingers surged into her hair and scraped against her scalp in a frenzied need that threatened to carry her into sheer bliss.

Almost as if he couldn't help it, his hips sought the cradle of her thighs. The potent evidence of his erection burned through his trousers and her thin Lycra. He pushed against her, a forceful presence that promised unlimited pleasure and infinite possibilities.

Possibilities…

Impossible!

With a hoarse cry she wrenched her lips from his.

He frowned, a dazed look in his eyes. 'Reiko?'

'Get off me,' she rasped, using every last ounce of her severely dwindled control to moderate her voice, to force back the panic as her senses reeled at what she'd almost let happen. How could she have been so foolish? How could she have let her guard down so completely?

The dazed look cleared from Damion's eyes. With lithe grace, he moved off her and sat with his back against the mirrored wall, one leg bent at the knee to hide the evidence of his arousal.

Somewhere in the confused miasma where her mind should have been, Reiko was thankful she couldn't see his erection. The thought of never again feeling him within her tore through her like a bullet.

'That shouldn't have happened. Although as pity kisses go, it wasn't half bad,' she said, once she was mid-way certain her voice would hold.

His gaze shot to hers. 'Is that what you think it was? A pity kiss?'

She shrugged and slowly sat up, grateful when her body cooperated. 'What else could it have been?'

She turned away before she could see his reaction. Belatedly remembering, she hurriedly attempted to brush her fringe over her scar—only to gasp when his hand shot out and captured hers.

'I've already seen your scar. Hiding it is pointless.'

'Tactlessness is a twenty-four-hour *malaise* for you, I see.'

She tried to free her arm. He easily restrained her, drew her closer and with his other hand brushed her hair away until the scar was completely exposed. Her breath caught as he slowly bent his head and touched his lips to her skin.

The feelings roiling through her were so tumultuous, so frightening, Reiko wanted to run and hide. With the last of her strength, she pushed him away.

'I'm certain I'll know who currently owns your painting within a day or two.' Any more time spent in Damion's presence was unthinkable. She'd find his precious painting as soon as possible or die trying! 'Once you're reunited with your painting, do me a favour and stay the hell away from me.'

CHAPTER SEVEN

GALLERIE FORTIER PARIS was also located in the third *arrondisse-ment*. The large former warehouse had been converted into a space that blended wood, glass and light in a jaw-dropping, stunningly beautiful design.

From the moment she entered, Reiko knew she'd stepped into a different world.

The exhibition was being held on the second floor of the three-floored gallery. Mounting the glass-and-steel staircase, Reiko couldn't help but feel envious that Damion got to come here to work every day. The display of spectacular art on each floor made the art-lover in her want to weep with joy.

She'd arrived early, and with Damion occupied with last-minute details, she took the opportunity to sneak a peek at the exhibition. At the door she accepted a glass of vintage champagne from a waiter, took a step into the room—and immediately knew why Damion had been so intent on acquiring the *Femme sur Plage*.

One entire wall had been dedicated to the works of Sylvain Fortier. Most of the paintings she'd never seen before, but a few stood out to her, her keen eye immediately recognising the subtle strokes and delicate colour combination that had made Damion's grandfather a renowned painter of his time.

In the middle of the wall the *Femme de la Voile*, another painting depicting Gabrielle Fortier, held pride of place. Although a delicate muslin veil covered most of her face, her eyes stared boldly at the painter, the intensity in their depths speaking of her power over the artist.

Reiko heard movement and turned. Damion stood behind her, his gaze focused on her. Her breath strangled in her throat as the memory of their kiss slammed into her. *Again.*

Dressed in a superbly cut tuxedo, with his slightly long hair brushed into place, he cut a powerfully dynamic figure, and the force of his sheer masculinity hit her like the slap of a Sirocco wind.

All day she'd been unable to take two steps without reliving those intense minutes on the gym mat. Heat rushed through her, making her blood surge faster, thicker through her veins. Between her legs, liquid warmth pulsed, as if readying her body for possession. Possession she knew would never happen.

'Reiko,' he murmured.

Her name sounded like a statement of ownership.

She wrenched her gaze away from his chest and turned back to the wall. 'You let me think this was a purely business venture. Why didn't you tell me you were holding the exhibition for your grandfather?'

'For the same reason you let me think you were involved with Ashton. Neither of us likes being caught off guard.' Beneath his tuxedo, powerful shoulders shrugged. 'And this is very personal to me.'

The simple admission and the desolate look on his face pierced through her.

'You wanted all three *Femme* paintings because they were your grandfather's first works?'

'*Oui.* They should be here—displayed together for him to see one last time.' The tight note to his voice told her how much it cost him to admit that.

Despite willing herself to feel nothing, a well of sympathy rose inside. 'I'm sorry.'

'*Merci,*' he breathed, continuing to stare at her with those intense grey eyes.

'So—'

'Where did you go this morning? You left before breakfast.' His tone held a note that made her insides clench. It sounded almost…possessive.

She indicated her soft grey mid-calf-length dress, her skin

tingling when his eyes followed the wave of her hand. 'I didn't pack anything suitable for the exhibition. I decided to head out early to find something before the rush.'

'You should've told me. I could've given you the name of a designer.'

Reiko felt a surge of something powerful and deeply unpleasant at the thought. She took a quick swallow of her champagne to wash it down. 'I'm glad I didn't. Isadora Baptiste's designs aren't quite my taste.'

Damion's eyes narrowed. 'You have something against her?'

'Can we pretend I know nothing but her name? Only you've got that cobra-about-to-pounce look right now.'

His gaze dropped to her lips, lingered, then returned to hers. 'I won't pounce. Not right now anyway.' His gaze travelled down her body, a frown materialising when he took in her four-inch grey platform shoes. 'You shouldn't be wearing those.'

'Excuse me?'

'With the amount of pain you were in last night, those heels are the last things you should be wearing.'

She wasn't sure whether to be offended or touched by his concern. 'Let me worry about what's good for me.'

'I don't understand why women torture themselves in the name of fashion. Those shoes are lethal. You shouldn't be wearing them.'

She raised her eyebrows. 'Considering you were a fashion designer's muse for a whole year, I'd think you of all people would grasp the concept.'

Over his shoulder she saw an old man being wheeled in, followed by the first trickle of guests. 'Your guests are arriving; I need to get to work.'

Frustration edged into his face. She started to turn away but he caught her hand. 'Reiko, we need to talk.'

'Sure. I'll catch up with you later.' She walked away quickly but could feel the force of his gaze at her back. Keeping the smile pasted on her face, she moved from painting to sculpture to 3-D display of abstract art, trying to let the magnificence of her surroundings wash away her bitterness.

What was it to her how Damion conducted his affairs, or how quickly he'd moved on from her into another woman's arms?

The knot of pain twisted inside her, mocking her pretended indifference. Barely a month after leaving her, Damion had been spotted with Isadora Baptiste, the married woman he'd slept with for a whole year. But who was she to be all high and mighty? Her behaviour after he'd left her had gouged a permanent groove of shame on her soul.

Lost in her painful haze, Reiko didn't realise she'd circled back to the original wall until she heard a heavy cough beside her.

The wheelchair-bound old man had a heavy blanket covering his knees. Despite his shock of white hair and shrunken features, there was a charisma with which he wore his snow-white tuxedo and black bowtie that felt vaguely familiar.

She watched him wheel his electric wheelchair closer to a frame that held flamboyant scrawled writing. Looking closer, Reiko saw that it was a poem—a simple but very powerful sonnet about love that brought a lump to her throat.

'Men are stupid.'

The bold statement caught her by surprise.

'We think we rule the world,' he continued in a thick French accent. 'We beat our chests, measure our dicks and crow when we think we have the biggest balls. But all comes to nothing in the face of a beautiful woman. A beautiful woman can make a man's dreams come true or destroy him with a simple flick of her smallest finger.' He turned his head and fixed piercing ice-blue eyes on her. 'Is that what you're doing to him?' He nodded to where Damion stood, surrounded by his guests.

Startled, Reiko quickly shook her head. 'Oh, no, you've got it wrong. There's nothing between—'

'That's what you're telling yourself right now. That's probably what *he's* telling himself. He's arrogant enough to think he holds all the cards. He always has been. But I can tell this time he's screwed.'

A bitter laugh escaped before she could stem it. 'Not by me,' she choked out, then felt heat rising in her face. 'I mean, I have no interest in screw…in attracting anyone. Not now. Not ever.'

He just smiled. 'Of course not. Because the last thing you want is him, correct?'

'Yes.'

His attention returned to the poem. 'Like I said—stupid,' he muttered.

His breath shuddered out, and his gaze was so intent on the words she felt as if she were intruding.

'We're all stupid, but given the choice we wouldn't change a thing.' He turned back to her. 'As you can probably tell, I won't be around much longer.'

Again the intensity in his eyes teased at her, reminding her of—

'I fear that my grandson will let my mistakes and his own past experiences get in the way of his happiness. But, should he be helped to see past those experiences, he will love deeply and completely.'

'Your grand—?' Reiko looked closer at the old man and everything fell into place. 'You're Sylvain Fortier,' she murmured. 'I'm so sorry. I didn't recognise you.'

The smile on his age-lined face was weary. 'I recognise you, *ma petite*. As I also recognise that certain decisions I took in the past may have impacted you.'

Reiko tried to swallow past the sudden lump in her throat. 'You're talking about my grandfather?'

Eyes very similar to Damion's bored into her. '*Oui*. If I ventured an apology, would it be well received?'

'It would certainly receive a fair hearing.' She glanced over to where Damion stood, surrounded by his guests.

'*Bon*, then I ask for your forgiveness. Although I think perhaps it is a different apology you require?'

Reiko opened her mouth to deny it but no sound emerged.

He nodded as if she'd answered him. 'Will you remember what I said about my grandson?'

More than a little dazed at the exchange, Reiko nodded. 'Um, yes. I will.'

Sylvain Fortier smiled. *'Bien. Au revoir.'*

Still reeling from the meeting, she wasn't prepared when she spotted her quarry several minutes later. Despite the slick veneer of his clothes, Reiko recognised Pascale Duvall instantly.

He stood beside a steel sculpture, a look of undisguised avarice on his face. Knowing how he'd acquired the jade figurine made her stomach turn, but she summoned a smile and approached him.

'Monsieur Duvall. I was hoping to run into you.' She introduced herself.

His wariness evaporated in the time it took for him to slide his gaze over her from top to toe. 'Mademoiselle Kagawa— a pleasure indeed.' He bent to kiss the back of her hand. Over his balding head she saw Damion shoot her a hard, dangerous look from where he stood beside his grandfather. Her nape tightened. Fearing he would guess why she'd wangled an invitation, she spoke quickly.

'I won't beat about the bush, Monsieur Duvall. Six months ago you were in Kyoto and came into possession of a jade figurine.'

The startled Frenchman started to release her hand. From the corner of her eye, she saw Damion heading towards her.

She held onto Duvall's hand and kept her gaze on his. 'The artefact belongs to my client. I want it back.'

'I paid a fair price for it—'

'No, you did *not*. It's a twelfth-century family heirloom worth at least twenty times what you paid for it. It was supposed to have been held until my client paid off her debt to a loan shark. He sold it to you at a fraction of the price for a quick profit.'

'That's not my problem.'

She tightened her grip. 'It should be. There was another buyer interested in the piece. He thinks you stole it from under his nose.' Reiko dropped the name of a well-known unscrupulous black-market dealer—one known to take very extreme measures in acquiring his art.

Pascale Duvall paled, his eyes growing wide.

She pressed home her advantage. 'You have two choices: sell the figurine back to me for what you bought it for, or I release your name to my circle of friends and you can deal with them. Either way, the piece won't be in your possession for very long.'

Damion drew level with her as she pressed her card into a shaken Duvall's hand. 'I'll wait to hear from you,' she murmured sweetly and released him.

'What the hell was that all about?' Damion demanded, his voice low and dangerous as he watched Duvall's hasty retreat.

She widened her eyes and let her smile broaden. 'Just doing my job while getting to know some of your friends.'

His eyes narrowed. 'If I find out that you're up to no good—'

She placed a finger on his lips, enjoying the sensation far more than she knew was safe for her. 'You're too suspicious for your own good. Relax or you'll develop ulcers.'

Damion's lips moved against her finger. If the thought wasn't absurd, she'd have believed he was caressing her finger with his lips. Fired up by the sensation as much as by the thought, she withdrew her finger and folded her hand into a fist.

'You spoke to my grandfather?'

She glanced warily over at Sylvain. 'Yes.' She bit her lip.

'What did he say to you?'

'He expressed his views on men and women—'

Recalling his exact words, she felt a blush climbing her face. And of course Damion saw it.

'How, exactly?' he asked in a lower, deeper voice.

'He said men were stupid—you won't get an argument from me there, by the way—and women rule the world. Then he said you and I were pretending we weren't attracted to each other—that given the chance we'd be tearing each other's clothes off and dance the Argentine tango naked.'

At his stunned look, she snorted. 'Relax, that last part was complete exaggeration on my part. By the way, I assured him there was no pretence, no attraction and definitely no tangoing.'

His eyes bored into hers. 'Did he believe you?'

'It doesn't matter what he believes. What you and I know is the truth is what matters, isn't it?'

Before he could answer, her phone trilled in her handbag. Pouncing on it with extreme relief, she answered it. A dart of surprise went through her when Pascale Duvall spoke. Her indication that she needed to take the call brought a dark frown to Damion's face. With a curt nod, he moved away.

Within minutes she'd arranged to take delivery of the figurine. Duvall's obvious reluctance to attract the attention of the Eastern European mobster was plain in his voice.

Once she'd concluded the call, she saw Damion had returned to his grandfather's side. Her pelvis throbbed with the dark promise of another painful night ahead if she didn't take off her shoes. Reiko made a quick decision.

The doorman was more than happy to pass her note to Damion and hail a taxi for her. Fabrice let her into the apartment. Within half an hour she was asleep on the sofa.

'Reiko, wake up.'

She fought her way through layers of disturbingly dark images to find Damion beside her, a grim look on his face.

'I…' She swallowed to ease her dry throat. 'What are you doing here?'

'Are you in pain?'

'No, I'm not.' The only thing causing her distress was the panic clawing through her, despite being fully awake.

His concern-etched frown didn't lessen. 'You were limping as you left the gallery.'

'Gee, and there I thought I had my swagger down to an art form.'

His jaw tightened. 'Why did you leave without me?'

'Because you're not my keeper. Go back to bed. I promise you there's no pain. I did my exercises before bed. I'm as nimble as an acrobat.' She swung her legs off the sofa, twisting away from the tangled sheets that bore testament to her tortured dreams.

He went to the drinks cabinet, poured a glass of water and handed it her. She took it from him, because to refuse felt rude.

'Do you have nightmares often?'

'I didn't have a nightmare.'

'Your screams say otherwise.'

She shrugged and lowered her head, unwilling for him to see the heat slowly crawling up her neck into her face. 'It's no big deal.'

'Why are you sleeping on the sofa?'

'It's more comfortable.'

He glanced pointedly at the sheets and pillow. 'Or you were hoping that I wouldn't hear when you screamed?'

Sitting down, he faced her, bringing his thigh to rest on the seat. With every fibre of her being, Reiko willed herself not to glance down at the hard muscle rippling beneath the cotton trousers.

'I don't know what you're talking about.'

'Yes, you do. You need help, Reiko.'

She tensed, anxiety and pain coursing through her in equal measures. 'Leave it, Damion. I don't want to talk about it.'

'Keeping it bottled up isn't healthy. Tell me why you think you're responsible for your father's death. I take it he was in the accident with you?'

'Why do I feel like I've visited this particular playground before?'

'We agreed to talk after the exhibition. You left before that could happen.'

'That should've been your first hint.'

'If it helps, I'll go first.'

Reiko realised she didn't want to know. Learning the sordid details of his affair so soon after he'd been with her diminished him somehow—made him less than the man who'd helped her last night in the gym and kissed her scar without showing any revulsion.

She took a hasty gulp of her water and set the glass aside. 'Only a few days ago you didn't even want to be in the same room as me. Now you want to know my life story.' She snorted. 'Seriously, the way you're acting, anyone would think you were hot for me.'

Her disbelieving laugh dried up when he just stared at her.

He didn't speak. Not one word. Yet the whole room boomed with the power of his thoughts.

She shook her head in confusion. 'You can't be. You walked away, remember?'

'I've told myself the same thing a few dozen times,' he clipped out. 'My conscience just laughs at me.'

'Try harder. You have a wife to find and little barons and baronesses to produce.'

His jaw tightened then released. 'In time, but not just yet.'

Her heart lurched. 'Nothing can come of it, and I won't be used to scratch a temporary itch.'

'Something already has come of it. Perhaps you need a refresher on our kiss last night?'

'Hell, Damion, this will never work. It… Things aren't that simple.'

'Explain.'

'I don't owe you any explanations.'

'Pascale Duvall left in a hurry. Did you have something to do with that?' His mercurial switch of subject threw her for a second.

She tried to keep her face and voice neutral. 'Maybe.'

He shoved a hand through his hair. 'We'll get nowhere if

you choose silence over talking. You're very talented, yet you choose to throw your talent away—'

'Whoa—that's *your* opinion. What I choose to do with my life is my business.'

'If I picked up the phone to the authorities right now, how interested would they be?'

Her heart hammered as she gauged the threat behind his statement. She licked her lips. 'On a scale of white to red, I'm a bright orange on their list.'

'Why?'

She shrugged when he raised his eyebrow, demanding an answer. 'They seem to think I feature in a few of their unsolved cases because of a trip I took to Mexico three years ago.'

'Do you?'

'Not in the way you think, no.'

'Then why not come clean? Silence can be construed as guilt.'

'I have nothing to prove to you or anyone. If the police had enough to charge me with, I'd be behind bars.'

'What if I asked you to come and work for me?'

Surprise shot through her. 'Why would you do that?'

'I'm always on the lookout for talent. You have it. You'd be paid handsomely.'

She didn't even think twice about it. Her life had taken a decidedly different turn after her accident. 'No, thank you.'

He shoved his hand through his hair again and Reiko fought a smile. The thought that she was riling him sent a sliver of satisfaction through her. It felt good to get under his skin the way he'd been getting under hers, both asleep and awake.

'What's so fascinating about the black market? Is it the danger?' His voice dripped with condemnation.

Reiko toyed with disclosing the true nature of her profession to him. Would he understand? He had everything. Immeasurable wealth, good looks, a title that dated back to medieval times. He only had to snap his fingers to have his every wish fulfilled.

Would he understand the need that drove people to hang onto one seemingly meaningless possession? Or spend their last cent retrieving the piece of history that made them who they were?

Taking a deep breath, she decided to give a little. 'After the First World War, a group of businessmen travelled through South East Asia, purportedly with the aim of setting up businesses that would employ thousands of people. But really what they wanted was to set up the illegal acquisition of art and artefacts. Twenty well-to-do families were targeted. Within five years the families' heirlooms had been completely depleted. They were left destitute. The jobs never materialised. Families were ripped apart.'

Retelling the story brought a hard lump of misery to her chest.

Picking up her glass, she took another sip. 'Most of them never recovered.'

When she chanced a glance at him, he compelled her to go on with a curt nod.

'My great-grandfather was not only one of those left with nothing—he was one of the people who convinced the other families to deal with the businessmen.'

'So how are you helping the families, exactly?'

'By recovering what was stolen from them and returning it to them.'

'A one-woman crusader—Robin Hood and a cat burglar rolled into one.' There was a lot less derision in his tone this time.

'Nothing so glamorous. I'm just very good at what I do.'

'Pascale Duvall—he's on your hit list.' It wasn't a question but a statement.

She couldn't see the harm in coming clean. 'Not any more. We've reached an agreement.'

Damion's gaze hardened. 'Aren't you afraid of repercussions?'

'Not as much as he's afraid of exposure.'

'You exploited his weak points?'

'I had a three-minute conversation with the man. If that displeases you, sue me.'

He fell silent, and the weight of his gaze on her set off an alarm that made her very aware that it was the middle of the night. Damion Fortier was in her room. There was a fit-for-hot-sex bed close by. And her attraction to him was off the scale.

The force of that thought released her other senses to go on a feeding frenzy. Sensations rushed at her. His scent hit her nostrils. Her ears picked up his steady breathing even as her eyes devoured him.

Only the sense of touch went unanswered. And even then her fingers tingled with the need to touch, to reacquaint herself with everything she'd trained herself to forget.

On cue, his gaze fell to her lips, his mouth parting slightly so she caught a tiny glimpse of his teeth and tongue.

She stopped breathing. Her pulse hammered through her ears, the rush of blood making her dizzy and thankful she was sitting.

'Damion—'

'Ask me anything you want.'

'What?'

'We agreed at the gallery we'd exchange information. Now it's your turn to ask me anything you want.'

She wanted to tell him to get lost. And she wanted to ask him a million questions. Reiko wasn't sure which she wanted more.

Heart suddenly racing, she licked her lips and saw his eyes darken in response.

'Did you love her?' The unplanned question broke the silence and slammed around the room like a living thing before coming to rest between them—a ticking grenade, ready to explode in her face.

'Did I *love* Isadora? *That's* what you want to know?' His voice held a thin sliver of ice that made her chest tighten. But he'd given her permission.

Jerkily, she nodded.

His lips firmed. 'No. I didn't love her.' The answer was delivered with a chilling finality that made her blood ice in her veins.

'Did she know that?'

'I was honest with her, but she chose to believe our agreement was…malleable.'

'So you were in it just for the sex?' Just as he'd been with her. Her chest tightened harder.

'I was seeking an escape. She provided it.'

'And that was all that mattered to you? *Your* escape?' Bitterness surged through her so forcefully she almost gasped with the strength of it. 'And when it became too much for you, you did what you do best—you tossed her aside and carried on your merry way, regardless of the trauma you'd left behind?'

Grey eyes darkened until they were almost black. One fist bunched on his thigh as he reined in control. For a second Reiko wondered whether she'd gone too far.

Then he exhaled slowly, long fingers flexing. 'I realise what it looks like from the outside. But appearances can be deceptive.'

'Trust me, I'm very well aware of that. But you just admitted you didn't love her, so it *appears* you were just in it for the sex. Must have been great sex, though, since you were with her for a whole year?' Whereas she'd merited a mere six weeks. Irrational anger seeped inside her, made her want to reach across the wide seat and smack him hard. Instead she surged to her feet.

He followed suit and stepped towards her. 'We're not done.'

She moved out of his reach. 'It's the middle of the night. We've had our little *tête-à-tête*—which, frankly, I don't see the point of.'

Lazy assurance gleamed in his eyes. 'It's a little more than a *tête-à-tête*, Reiko. What we have is as strong as ever. Don't deny you feel it, too.'

Pain punched through her. 'Even if I felt remotely like you do—which I don't—there won't be a repeat of what happened between us five years ago. Not in this lifetime.'

His eyes narrowed, his stance gaining a determination that sent alarm skittering through her.

'You seem so very convinced. But I've held you in my arms. Your body was telling a different story last night.'

'You caught me at a weak moment.'

'The trouble with weak moments, *cherie*, is that they have a habit of recurring. With enough encouragement they can recur with mind-boggling frequency.'

As if to demonstrate, he reached out for her. But she'd been prepared for it and jumped out of his reach.

Surprise lit his eyes. 'Maybe you are a ninja after all.' The amusement in his voice made her pulse race faster. 'You don't care for a demonstration?'

'No, I don't.'

'Don't trust yourself?'

'I'm just trying to save you time and effort. You won't want me, Damion.'

Perhaps it was the finality in her voice. Perhaps it was the heavy trace of bitter weariness she didn't manage to hold back.

He froze, his eyes narrowing intently on her. 'Why not?'

'Because even if I wanted to, Damion, I can't sleep with you. I'm incapable of having sex.'

CHAPTER EIGHT

JAPAN IN LATE FEBRUARY was beautiful. As a native, she was deeply biased. But even the most critical eye couldn't fault the impending promise of spring, the fresh, crisp air or the general buzz of renewed energy in the people around her.

'Arigato.' She took her passport from the immigration officer and made her way through the VIP exit of Itami Airport, very conscious of the imposing man beside her.

Reiko breathed in deeply, her sense of homecoming so acute she stopped in her tracks just outside the doors leading out of the airport.

A warm hand arrived at her back as Damion stopped beside her. 'Are you okay?'

Keeping her gaze averted from his heavy, puzzled stare, she nodded. 'Better than okay. It's good to be home.'

In the twenty-four hours since she'd dropped her bombshell, she'd felt that look over and over. Even when she'd pretended to be tired during their flight and sought the insanely luxurious comfort of the private jet's divan, she'd felt his gaze on her.

What surprised her was that he hadn't tried to prise the information out of her the way he'd tried to dig into everything else in her life.

The thought that he'd lost interest that quickly, that he was willing to move on to another, more palatable target, should have pleased her. Instead it reminded her again of how easily he'd walked away five years ago.

She pushed the painful thought to the back of her mind as a black limousine swung into the kerb in front of her.

Again she felt the heat of Damion's hand as he pushed her towards it.

'Wait—what are you doing?'

A droll expression flashed across his face. 'I thought it was obvious. We're getting into the car.'

'You may be. I'm not. I'll get a taxi. My apartment is only ten minutes away.'

'You're not staying at your apartment.' His hand propelled her towards the car.

'Don't tell me—you just happen to own a penthouse suite in town, right?'

'Naturally. I do a lot of business all over Japan. Besides, we have an agreement. Until the painting is in my possession, you remain with me.'

When her contact had informed her that he'd traced the *Femme sur Plage* to a Japanese collector, she'd hoped for a quick dissolution of their association. Instead his insistence that she finish the job had brought a foolish little bubble of pleasure even as the fear that he would uncover her secrets grew in direct proportion.

'So if I had to go and feed my imaginary goldfish, you wouldn't let me go?'

'I'd come with you. I'm quite interested to see these fish for myself.'

She laughed. Just like that. The action took her by surprise. It seemed to take him by surprise, too, because his eyes widened right before a smile lifted his sensual mouth.

Reiko let herself be propelled forward. The driver opened the door for her. Just before she got in, she felt Damion move closer. His breath brushed against the shell of her ear. 'I also haven't forgotten that bombshell you dropped last night. You now owe me several explanations, *ma fleur*. So you're not going to get away from me that easily.'

Icy dread snapped through her as she slid into the car. He got in behind her, his gaze intent on her face as the limo joined the smooth traffic.

Several emotions were coursing through her, none of which

she could readily vocalise. Finally, she glanced at him. 'I thought you'd given up on m—on pursuing that particular subject.'

The smile that curved his sensual mouth held the steel of determination. 'Last night you were tired and distressed and clearly needed a reprieve. Don't mistake reprieve for uninterest. I haven't given up on you. Not by a long shot.'

Her breath quickened and she called herself ten kinds of fool for not running in the other direction. Once Damion knew the true extent of how damaged she was, he would be the one doing the running. Of that she had no doubt.

'This boundary thing isn't really a problem for you, is it?'

He grinned, flashing even white teeth that made him look years younger than his thirty-five. It also caused her heart to skitter in her chest like a rabbit on steroids.

'Five years ago our chemistry was insane. Despite your curious desire to run from it, it's still there. What you said was equivalent to tossing a grenade in my lap. Do you blame me for wanting to do something about that? What would you do in my place?'

A reluctant smile tugged at her lips. 'I'd chuck it out the nearest window and run like hell.' Recalling just what it was they were discussing, she sobered. 'I don't know why you're intent on pursuing this, but I'm truly not the woman you knew five years ago, Damion.'

His smile slowly faded. 'No, you're not. But perhaps I may have misjudged you.'

She felt a sharp kick under her ribcage. 'You didn't. I took your money—'

'Then promptly gave it away to charity.'

Her mouth dropped open, then snapped shut. 'Don't make me out to be a paragon, Damion. I'm as contemptible as you think I am.' The things she'd done after he'd walked away...

He inhaled sharply. 'We've both done things we're not proud of, but nothing is unforgivable.'

The sudden lump in her throat made talking impossible so

she just shook her head. When the pressure of his gaze got to be too much, she looked out of the window. Immediately she felt soothed by Kyoto's familiar landmarks.

The Imperial Palace and the Nijo Castle, even the mild stench from Nishiki Market imbued a sense of homecoming so strong, tears threatened.

'So what's the plan?' Damion's deep voice roused her from musings.

As if on cue, her phone buzzed with an incoming message. With relief, she activated it and read the message.

'We're going clubbing.'

He paced the vast living room of his penthouse, forcing himself not to check his watch for the umpteenth time. They were supposed to have left fifteen minutes ago.

The last thing he wanted was to go out, especially in light of the latest morsel Reiko had revealed. What he really wanted to do was lock her up in a room and interrogate her until every last secret she was hiding was out in the open.

But he knew he couldn't do that. Thoughts of Isadora intruded. The hard stance he'd taken when he'd discovered just what she was hiding from him had reaped disastrous consequences. He couldn't afford to do that with Reiko.

Why is this so important to you?

Damion shied away from the persistent voice and glanced at his watch again.

Why was she taking so long? What was so damned special about where they were going that she had to make this much effort with her appearance?

Recalling the smile on her face after she'd read the text, he clenched his jaw. Without realising he was moving, he stood in front of her door, his fist rapping on the polished wood.

She pulled the door open. 'Hold your horses. I'm ready…'

The sudden drumming in his ears drowned out the rest of her words.

Her dress was blood-red threaded with gold. The high collar and wide, long sleeves clearly lent themselves to a traditional geisha look that was destined to ensnare the interest of every red-blooded male with a ten-mile radius.

But it was the plunging neckline that hit him like a punch in the solar plexus. The very smooth, very tempting slopes of her breasts made heat surge through his groin. He felt himself harden long before the seductive scent from her sinfully voluptuous body reached his nostrils. His fist suspended in the air, he swallowed thickly.

'Damion?'

'Oui?' he managed past the haze of lust that threatened to unman him.

She licked her lips and his fever rose another dangerous notch.

'I said, are you okay?'

He felt his frown return, but this time impatience at being kept waiting had nothing to do with his pique. *'Naturellement.* Why shouldn't I be?'

When she shrugged, his gaze fell back to the semi-exposed curve of one plump breast. 'Are you wearing a coat over that dress?'

Her perfectly plucked brow rose. 'It's warm out. I don't need a coat.'

He wanted to argue with that but held off. *'Bien,* let's go.'

He was about to turn and head for the door when her saucy smile stopped him in his tracks.

'Quoi?'

'You probably don't play poker, but if you ever decide to take it up, I think you should know you have a tell.'

'A *tell?'*

She nodded. 'You slip into French when you're agitated. Although why you're agitated right now is beyond me.'

'Is it?'

Damion deliberately let his gaze drop to linger over her face, her red-painted mouth, her sinfully delicious cleavage. He took his time, let his eyes feast on her. Then he met her eyes. Her skin held the distinct beginnings of a flush.

Remembering the way her eyes darkened when she was aroused, as they were doing now, he swallowed hard. 'Now that we've established the reason for my agitation, shall we go?'

'I… of course…but…'

'No more buts. You've thrown enough obstacles in my way. Let's go and get this over with. *Then* we'll deal with the buts.'

'I'm sure there's a saying somewhere about arrogance and bullheadedness.'

'We can add it to the many subjects to discuss later.' He held out his arm to her. After a second's hesitation, she took it. Satisfaction oozed through him. When her fingers found his forearm, Damion's pulse jumped.

Within seconds each and every muscle in his body tautened with need. He'd woken up this morning in the same state, his senses on high alert, as if held on a knife-edge of heady possibility.

A part of him still resented her for taking another man to her bed so soon after him. But he'd realised during the course of a long, restless night that he risked hypocrisy since he'd done the same with Isadora mere weeks after leaving Reiko.

The whole situation between them had been handled badly. He aimed to fix it.

As for that nonsense about being incapable of having sex… Reiko oozed sex. If she thought that would throw him off, she would find out just how mistaken she was.

Reiko Kagawa wanted him with the same intensity he wanted her. And he intended to make her face the reality of *them* tonight.

The nightclub was located in Gion District, famous for its geisha interests. One look out of the window at the row of shabby warehouses and Damion was ready to tell the driver to keep driving. The grunge-wearing clubbers were so far removed from the members of the private gentlemen's club and the exclusive social circles he moved in it was beyond hilarious.

His gaze swung back inside the car when Reiko sat forward and rapped on the closed partition.

When his driver pulled over, Damion frowned at her. 'What are you doing?'

She ignored him and went for the door handle. 'We'll walk from here.'

'No, we won't. This is a dangerous neighbourhood.'

She merely raised an eyebrow at him. 'Scared?'

'Selectively risk averse.'

'Club Caramel is just around the corner. If you pull up in a money-bags car like this, we won't be allowed in.'

'That makes no sense whatsoever.'

'I know, but trust me.' She flung open the door and stepped out.

Damion's gaze dropped to her feet and he breathed a sigh of relief when he saw she'd chosen more sensible-heeled shoes tonight. Although the red ties criss-crossing their way up her firm calves to end in saucy little bows made breathing an extremely trying exercise. Just as the thought of abandoning his car exercised any common sense.

He followed her out, but before he could question her she'd dismissed his driver and was pulling him along the kerb.

'Now, remember what happens in *Fight Club*…' She reached up and sank her fingers into his hair, and the rest of her words dissolved under the force of desire that punched through his gut.

'*Qu'est que tu fais?* What are you doing?' he translated hoarsely when he noted he'd lapsed into his mother tongue.

She continued to muss his hair, teasing her fingers through it in a way that turned him on so hard he barely bit back a growl.

He firmly took hold of her wrist. 'I'm perfectly presentable.'

She looked him up and down. 'That's the problem. You look like a billion dollars.'

'Only a billion?'

Her brown eyes rolled. Damion knew his libido was in danger of skidding way out of control when he remembered just how sexy he found that.

'I know you're worth several more. I just don't want to advertise it.'

'And making me look unkempt is your answer?' he asked.

'I'm aiming for grungy rich, not filthy rich.'

'Your contact has something against money?'

'Only the need to part you from as much of it as possible once he realises who you are.'

He started to shrug, but stopped when she placed her hand on his chest.

As usual, the simple act of her touch on him had the effect of stopping him dead in his tracks. He tried to breathe but only managed an inadequate puff.

She tugged up the collar of his leather jacket. 'Okay, you're ready.'

He nodded, unable to tear his eyes from her glossy lips.

'Oh, and, Damion…?'

'Oui?' he rasped.

'Let me do the talking, okay?'

Reiko sipped her drink and tried not to look to her right where Damion, the buttons of his jacket open to display his broad, black-shirted chest and entirely too-sexy body, was indeed letting her do the talking—albeit in a very distracting way.

When his forceful stare got to be too much, she swung her head towards him and raised her eyebrows. *What do you think you're doing?* A slow, supremely sexy smile curved his lips and he stretched back further in his seat, his arm moving lazily along the back of it. His fingers grazed her arm, and she nearly jumped out of her skin.

Opposite her, Yoshi Yamamoto, her friend and contact in all things art, smirked.

'What are you smirking at?' she demanded in Japanese, desperately willing her pulse rate down.

His smile widened. 'I've known you since you were six, Rei. I've never seen you this rattled by anyone—let alone a stuffy ex.'

Heat crept up her neck and she was thankful the club was dark enough to disguise it. 'Shut up! I'm not all shook up. And he's not stuffy. He…he's French.'

'He also looks like he can drop a few million on some German art I've come into possession of. Care to broker a deal? I'll split the commission with you.'

'He's not interested. And don't underestimate him. He'll see right through you.'

He grinned. 'Wow, you're defending him. I guess it's true what they say—there's a thin line between lust and lust.'

'That's not what—' She huffed. 'I didn't come here for you to take cheap shots at my personal life, Yosh. Do you have the information I need?'

Yoshi sobered and nodded. Beside her, Reiko thought she felt Damion stiffen, but when she slid a glance at him, he looked as relaxed as ever.

'It surfaced again a few weeks ago, when lover-boy here started hunting for it. Word on the street is he's willing to pay whatever it takes to get it back.' His gaze drifted to Damion and returned to hers. 'I guess him being here confirms it?'

Reiko waved away his interest. 'Why didn't you call me?'

He frowned. 'You told me you'd retired.'

'Do you have the buyer's details?'

Yoshi tapped his phone. 'I'm expecting a call in the next fifteen minutes with that information.'

A provocatively dressed woman approached their table and sank down next to Yoshi. She played with his hair and he absently rubbed her thigh. But the woman's gaze kept straying to Damion, and the very keen interest in her eyes made Reiko's insides clench with a powerfully dangerous emotion.

Recognising it as possessiveness, she felt her breath snag in her throat. She darted her gaze to Damion, fearful he'd somehow guessed, and found him watching her with focussed intensity.

'With the crazy currents flying between you two, I'd say get a room—but, since this is a respectable club, why don't you go dance with your man before I drown in all that *sexual tension*?' Yoshi said suggestively, his tone amused as he pulled his girlfriend closer into his lap. 'I'll come find you when the call comes.'

'I think that's a great idea,' Damion replied in perfect, exquisite Japanese.

Reiko gaped at him. Yoshi's laughter and his *'Well played, my friend'* barely registered because she was frantically replaying everything she'd said since they got here.

Oh, God!

When Damion caught hold of her wrist and pulled her up, she followed him onto the dance floor, still in a daze.

His amusement as he pulled her close finally loosened her tongue.

'You. Speak. Japanese. It's epically sneaky of you not to tell me.'

'I told you I do a lot of business in Japan. And I think you know me well enough to know I don't like to relinquish the upper hand.'

'You still could've told me you understood everything I said back there.'

'You told me to let you do the talking, remember?'

She had no answer for that. She was too busy kicking herself for making assumptions where Damion was concerned.

A particularly energetic couple danced close. Damion caught her around the waist and lifted her out of their way. 'So…I'm not stuffy—I'm…French?'

Heat stung her cheeks. 'I was trying to be polite. I shouldn't have bothered.'

'What would you have called me if you knew I could understand you?'

'Arrogant, opinionated, pushy as all hell.'

Low, deep laughter rumbled through his chest. This close, she could feel the heat rising from his body. And the ease with which he moved.

Damion Fortier, the French aristocrat she'd assumed wouldn't fit into this strange, alternative world, danced just as in her dream. The grace and precision of his feet as he moved to the beat, the supple abandon in his hips and the arrogant confidence with which he danced soon drew eyes to them. Remembering how heated their dance had become in her dreams, Reiko felt her insides clench with need.

She tried to look away from him but found she couldn't. His sheer animal magnetism held her captive.

They danced for what seemed like hours but in reality was barely ten minutes.

'You're exceptionally good,' he murmured against her earlobe. 'I should've taken you dancing five years ago.'

The reminder had the effect of cold water thrown in her face. 'You should've done a lot of things five years ago.'

She stepped away from him but Damion caught her back easily. He ignored her glare and nodded towards the VIP lounge.

'I think your friend has the details for us.'

On the way back to their seats, his arm came around her and pulled her closer. The heat of him short-circuited her brain. She was still scrambling madly when Yoshi pulled a piece of paper from his pocket.

Damion took it before she could, and thanked Yoshi in flawless Japanese. Struggling to focus, Reiko reached out with the intention of touching her friend—only to find her hand captured in Damion's. This time Yoshi's smile held heavy circumspection.

Without breaking off his conversation, Damion tucked her hand through his arm and pulled her to his side. The move felt so familiar and natural she was stunned by the temptation to ease into it.

The power of that emotion frightened her into pulling away. A small frown creased his eyebrows, but aside from that small betrayal of emotion, Damion didn't react. He carried on talking, but she could tell he was attuned to her every move.

Forcing in a deep breath, she smiled at Yoshi. 'Thanks for your help, Yosh.'

He waved her away. 'I owed you for giving me the heads-up about the Qianlong vase two months ago. Consider this a freebie.'

Damion handed him his card. 'I'm always interested in new pieces. If that German art is all above board, contact my gallery.'

Yoshi let out an appreciative whistle and tucked the card into his pocket. With a wave, he melted into the heaving crowd.

Feeling desperately out of kilter, Reiko headed towards the bar.

'Tequila.'

'Make that two,' Damion ordered, peering down at her with those intense eyes.

When two shots of tequila were slid in front of her, she picked one up and downed it with a shudder.

'Do you feel better?' Damion enquired, sipping his.

'Nope.'

His features tightened. 'It's time to go.' He guided her out with a hand in the small of her back. His car was waiting at the kerb and she slid in without protest.

As they pulled away, his gaze stayed on her. 'Did you have a thing with him?'

Her breath caught. 'With who?'

'Yoshi Yamamoto.'

'He's my friend.'

'That doesn't answer my question. It's very easy. Yes or no?' A dangerous edge lined his voice.

He'd completely morphed from attentive companion and

incredible dancer to an iceman whose eyes threatened to peel the skin from her flesh.

'The answer is no. I've known him since we were kids. We're just friends.'

'Good,' he rasped.

'So, what? Now you're jealous?' she asked, incredulous.

'I'm a possessive man. I don't relinquish what is mine.' He locked gazes with her, the force of his will rushing down on her like a thunderbolt from the sky. *'Ever.'*

The statement, simple in itself, was made with such gravity, such intense foreboding, that it sent a heavy pulse of apprehension through her.

Reiko stared at him, unable to look away despite the dangerous swirling emotions within her depths. He didn't speak for several minutes. His gaze traced over her face, down her body, to the fingers she was twisting in her lap.

'I've frightened you.'

She let out a hoarse laugh and shook her head. 'You were intense before—just not this intense. It's not frightening. It's…'

'A turn-on? The thought of being possessed by me again?'

The delicious thrill that went through her shamed and excited her even as she was pushing both feelings away. Damion would never possess her again.

'Since that'll never happen again, this is a moot point, isn't it?'

'Never is a delicious challenge at the best of times. When it has the discourtesy to come wrapped in something I really, *really* want…' The rest of his words dangled tantalisingly out of reach. Then he added a Gallic shrug.

Her unravelling started with a force of melting heat rushing through her. Followed by the stinging puckering of her nipples. Damion smiled, as if he knew the effect he was having on her.

He captured her hand and raised it to his lips. Warm, firm, his kiss branded her.

'Don't be frightened, *ma petite*. This time will be even better than the first.'

'First of all, don't call me that. I'm not your little anything. Secondly, nothing is going to happen between us.' Nothing could. It was impossible. 'Besides, have you forgotten you have to find a future baroness soon? Tick-tock, my friend. Don't waste your time on a conquest that has no meaning for you. You should be out there finding yourself a wife before you go extinct.'

Why did saying that scrape her throat and scour her heart so painfully?

His smile didn't disappear, but Reiko sensed the change in the atmosphere—a sudden chill, as if she'd struck a nerve. Thankfully the car pulled up at his penthouse.

Damion set her free and she alighted.

Once they were back in his penthouse, she turned towards the hallway. 'I think I've stayed up long enough to reduce the worst of the jet lag, so I'll head to bed now.'

'Running away?' he taunted softly.

'Retreating. Like the very wise ninja that I am.'

'What's between us isn't going to go away.'

'Wanna bet?'

His jaw tightened. 'It isn't a game.'

'No, it isn't. Which is why you should let it go. Pursue it and you'll end up very disappointed. I've told you that over and over. Why won't you listen to me?'

Shrugging out of his jacket, he flung it over the back of a chair. The breadth of his shoulders and the sheer physical power in his movements threatened to further melt her brain. So, despite her intention to retreat, she remained rooted to the spot as he rounded the sofa and grabbed her arms. The heat that never stayed banked when he was near flared to roaring life inside her.

'Because you haven't given me a good reason to. What did you mean by you can't have sex?' His thumbs rubbed back and forth, causing a low moan to rise within her.

Ruthlessly, she bit it down. 'Maybe I'm into girls now?'

His rich, throaty laugh made her pulse race faster.

'No, *cherie*, you most certainly are not into girls. You're into men. More specifically, you're into *me*. So much so, your whole body vibrates with the sensations I cause inside you. Try again.'

Impossibly, Reiko began to waver. 'You think you're so good at this, don't you?'

He frowned. 'Good at what?'

'The relentless battering. You think you can wear me down.'

His frown cleared. 'We both want the same thing.'

'No!' Reiko shouted, cursing under her breath when her voice emerged wobbly and tear-soaked. 'Believe me, we don't.'

'Why? What would happen if you gave in to me?'

'I can't.' She knew without a shadow of a doubt that she would never survive revealing herself to Damion only to have him walk away from her again.

She trembled when he cupped her face in his hands. Transfixed, she watched his head descend, the promise of his firm, pleasure-giving lips drawing ever closer. She clenched her fists, clamping them to her sides to keep from touching him the way every fibre of her being yearned to.

His lips seared over hers. Her moan broke free. With a soft grunt of satisfaction Damion deepened the kiss, sliding one hand behind her head to hold her in place while the other performed the same task around her waist, bringing her close to his hard, whipcord body. Securing her exactly where he wanted her, he set about giving her a blistering demonstration of just how good he was.

Within moments Reiko's lips opened beneath his, inviting the bold invasion of his tongue, which he swept through without mercy. She whimpered, the need to touch him a fever raging through her blood.

But at the back of her mind, she knew that was the one thing saving her from giving in totally to this madness. Touch had become her one saviour. Touch grounded her, anchored her to reality. At least it had until she'd met Damion again. Now he'd stripped even that safe anchor from her. Now she knew the moment she touched him she would be swept away. And she couldn't afford to be swept away—couldn't afford the wrenching heartache that would come with exposing herself to him.

Sensing he'd lost some of his potent connection, Damion pulled back a fraction. His mouth didn't completely leave hers but she felt him stiffen slightly.

'Reiko?' he rasped against her lips.

'Let me go.'

'Did I hurt you?' His tone held a trace of puzzlement.

'Please, just let me go.'

'Tell me—'

'I'm exhausted. My body clock is on stupid o'clock. I don't have any fight left in me and I have an early-morning meeting. You can probably push me into telling you my darkest secret, but I'm hoping you won't because it won't be a fair fight.'

Slowly his lips left hers, followed by his hands, then the warmth of his body. Regret pierced her heart but she forced herself to accept it.

Regret was good. It built character.

Regret is also a lonely bedfellow.

Shut up!

'You'll tell me one day very soon—*without* the need for torture instruments.'

She finally opened her eyes and returned his passion-heavy stare. 'You really are cocky, aren't you?'

He merely shrugged.

'Okay…umm…good luck with that.' She backed up until she was inside the door. 'Goodnight.'

Turning, she fled.

CHAPTER NINE

'HOW GOOD ARE your contacts in Eastern Europe?' Damion asked from across the breakfast bar, where he was finishing his coffee.

She looked up from the box containing the jade figurine she'd retrieved from Pascale Duvall. 'The best in the business. Why?'

His gaze dropped to the figurine and back to her face. 'I want you to reconsider my job offer.' He raised his hand when she started to protest. 'On a contract basis. I'm thinking of branching into Eastern Europe. My sources took far too long to locate the rightful owners of the Matryoshka dolls. Use your contacts to verify the pedigree of the pieces I acquire.'

'You must have a thousand employees who can do that for you.'

'One thousand and one has a nice ring to it.'

He named the price of her employment and her mouth dropped open. That sort of money would make a huge difference to the lives of so many in her support group.

When he reached over and tugged her chin up with one long finger, heat stole through her, followed closely by suspicion.

'You wouldn't happen to be making this offer because you're hoping I'll end up in your bed, would you?'

'You'll end up there whether you take the job or not.'

His sheer audacity stole her breath away. She didn't bother to argue with him because she was beginning to recognise the futility of it. Instead she picked up the box, grabbed her bag and headed for the door. He was there before her, opening the door for her, a look in his eyes that made her alternately want to keep staring into those grey depths and run and hide.

She didn't want to be the focus of Damion's attention. And yet she wasn't running in the opposite direction as she ought to.

He smiled, and a shiver, delicious and intense, washed over her. Desperately she pushed it away. She couldn't afford to let her guard down where Damion was concerned. The woman he thought he was pursuing no longer existed.

'Keep building those barriers against me,' he drawled. 'I'll take great pleasure in knocking them down.'

'I wasn't building barriers. I was considering your job offer.'

He took the box from her and led her through the lobby towards the car. 'And?'

'I'm leaning towards yes.'

He smiled. *'Bravo, ma cherie.'*

'What's that supposed to mean?'

'It means you're not as afraid of this thing between us as I thought.'

'Or it could be that that I can't resist fattening my bank account with easy money.'

Damion waved away his driver and opened the door himself. Once they were in the car, he stashed the box on the seat across from them, reached across and pulled her body into his.

'If you're trying to put me off by making me think you're mercenary, don't forget I know what you did with the million dollars. If I had to guess, I'd say it's probably what you intend to do with the commission money, and why you've liquidated most of your assets.'

Her stunned gasp earned a smug smile.

'You've just confirmed it. What is it, exactly?' he asked.

She licked her lips. 'It's a fund for victims of natural and man-made disasters,' she murmured.

For several seconds he said nothing. Then he curved his fingers around her nape and yanked her against his body. His kiss was every bit as devastating as it had been last night, every bit as mind-melting. When he cupped her breast, the sensation was so powerful, so intensely arousing, she wanted to crawl into his lap and demand more. Instead she forced herself to pull back.

Darkened eyes stared at her from a face carved with arousal before they dropped to linger on her lips.

'What was that?' she asked through lips that tingled wildly.

'A kiss. One of many that will form part of my artillery.'

She squeezed her eyes shut as her breath shuddered out. Even when he grasped her hand and trailed a path of kisses over it, she couldn't bring herself to open her eyes. The weakening in her belly told her she'd need all of her reserves to fight what Damion seemed bent on doing to her.

'Can we just go, please? I don't want to be late.'

'*Certainement*. Give me the address.'

She read it out to him and he passed it to the driver. For the hour-long drive to the crisis centre where she was meeting her client, Damion kept hold of her hand. Every time she tried to pull it back, he tightened his grip. In the end, she allowed him to keep it.

Returning the jade figurine that had been in her client's family for countless generations brought a lump to Reiko's throat that remained there long after she'd left the very grateful client behind.

She felt Damion's heavy gaze on her before he spoke. 'You've just proved my point.'

'What point?'

'That you don't do this for the money.'

She shrugged. 'I gave her my word that I'd find and return what was taken from her. She trusted me. I wasn't about to let her down.'

'Who do *you* trust, Reiko?'

'Excuse me?'

'If you trusted enough to share, you wouldn't be carrying that rock of pain inside you.'

She inhaled sharply, the depth of the pain that lanced through her stealing her breath. 'How dare you?'

'You're keeping me at bay because you're afraid to trust your instinct.'

'You threatened Trevor and me with jail unless you got your way. Five years ago you walked away from me without a backward glance. You think I ought to just drop everything and trust you?'

'I've kept my end of the bargain—I've left Ashton alone. As of this morning, the balance of his debt is zero.'

Surprise shot through her. 'You… Why would you do that?'

'With you in jail, I don't get what I want. And I want you.'

'You paid off Trevor's debts in the hopes of getting into my pants?'

A distasteful look crossed his face. 'There's *your* tell. When you feel backed into a corner, you become crude. Some men might find that sexy—'

'But you don't?'

'I'm more concerned with the why. You were downing tequila shots last night because you can't handle what is happening between us.'

Forcefully, she pulled away from him. This time he let her go. 'Downing shots is way better than *your* alternative!'

He stiffened. 'What's that supposed to mean?'

'You had a year-long affair with a married woman. *A married woman with children!*' The depth of her disgust rose like bile within her.

His hauntingly beautiful face hardened, his cheekbones standing out so prominently, he seemed hewn from marble. 'Don't presume to think you know—'

'Oh, please! Everyone knows you destroyed Isadora Baptiste's marriage, then discarded her when it suited you. Is it true you wouldn't let her see her children for six whole months?'

His jaw clenched. 'No. That's not true.'

'You can have any woman you want, Damion. Why would you break a family apart like that?' Her throat felt raw.

'I didn't—'

'You know what? This really isn't any of my business. Just like my life is none of yours.' Rapping on the partition, she asked the driver to pull over.

'What the hell are you doing?' he demanded.

'I have a sudden urge to feed my goldfish. I don't know when I'll be back, so don't wait up for me.'

Stepping out, she struck out blindly—just plunged into the throng of people and let them carry her. She didn't realise where she was until she heard the eerie, hauntingly familiar sound of an approaching train.

Desperately she tried to step back. Panic clawed at her insides. A scream scrambled to get out despite her every effort to keep it down.

The train arrived and she felt herself being pushed forward. *No!*

Almost as if she had no control over her limbs, Reiko went with the crowd…and stepped onto the train.

Paralysed with fear, she clung to the nearest pole. She wouldn't break down. She couldn't. They'd arrive at the next stop in minutes.

Think about something else.

Taking huge gulps to calm her nerves, she scrambled around—and shut her eyes with a sense of inevitability when her mind alighted on its favourite subject.

Damion.

Ever since Damion had crashed his way into Trevor's house and back into her life, she hadn't been able to take a full breath. Her body and mind felt on edge, as if she was on a roller coaster that was speeding faster and faster, every sign pointing to its careening out of control. And, try as she might, she couldn't find the 'off' button.

This is crazy.

'It's nothing compared to what will happen if you ever run from me like that again.' The deep, quietly livid tones of the man haunting her made her already hammering heart skitter out of control.

Reiko swivelled to find him behind her, molten grey eyes glaring down her, his chest heaving as if he'd ran a marathon.

She wanted to demand why he'd followed her, why he was in her head so she couldn't think of anything else. But she knew if she dared to open her mouth her whole world would collapse. So she stared up at him, fighting just to keep breathing. Frantically, she searched for the countdown to the next stop.

'Don't think I will hesitate to restrain you if you try to run from me again.'

Reiko didn't doubt he meant it. But staying on the train was so much worse than Damion's threats. Distressed, she bit her lip. His gaze dropped to her mouth, then rose to rake her face. His dark frown intensified.

'Reiko? Are you okay?'

Lips clamped shut, she desperately shook her head.

His arm surrounded her immediately, caging her in his protective warmth. The scent of his aftershave filled her nostrils. Helplessly needing him, she clung to him for dear life. His arms tightened around her and she raised her head to look at him.

He stared right back at her, then gave a grim smile. 'We'll go and feed your fish. Then we'll talk. No excuses this time. It's time to remove these barriers between us once and for all.'

Damion barely succeeded in hiding his relief when she sagged into him, but his insides clenched with the knowledge that something was seriously wrong with Reiko. Her face was pale and her grip tightened on his jacket at the barest movement of the train. Confusion rumbled through him.

There had never been a choice as to whether he'd follow her or not. In fact the need had been so visceral he hadn't paused a millisecond to examine it. His head of security would probably be having a coronary, because Damion was sure the team hadn't made the train. *He'd* barely made it.

He, who'd never chased a woman in his life, who took pains to extricate himself from a liaison at the first sign of clinginess, had just chased a woman down a heaving subway and through several train carriages, a chasm of fear gaping wide at the thought that he'd lost her.

She cast furtive glances at him. He remained silent. He needed time to process exactly what was going on inside him.

His gaze wandered over her slightly parted lips, the wide, beautifully shaped eyes, the wild abandon of her hair, the small but perfectly shaped body, the thin edge of the scar that ended beside her right ear.

He wanted her as he'd never wanted another woman—so much so his insides quaked with the thought of not having her.

What he didn't understand was *why*. He'd taken steps never to associate himself with the sort of woman he'd found Reiko out to be shortly after he'd walked away. Women like his mother, and especially his grandmother, who'd created so much unhappiness in his own childhood.

And yet here he was…

'How many more stops?' he asked, absently noting that his voice wasn't quite as steady as he wanted it to be. He wanted to get off the train. To drag her into a distant cave, look into her eyes and uncover her every last secret. He wanted no secrets between them.

He'd pretended Isadora's secrets were harmless until it had been too late…

'One more.'

'Do you live alone?' The sudden thought that she might not hit him with a force of a tornado.

'No, I have a boy toy tied to my bed. You'd just be cramping our—'

He grabbed her chin and shut her up the best way he knew how. Her breath whooshed into his mouth, sending a hot tide of want surging through him. Damion didn't care where they were or who was watching. The kiss fired up his whole body, making him yearn, making him crave her…

Mon Dieu, it was almost as if…as if…he was *obsessed*.

He jerked back from her, a sudden chill slamming through his need. His head reeled.

Her eyes widened, looking up at him with an almost frightened expression. He wanted to tell her not to be frightened but he knew he couldn't make such an assurance.

The train pulled into the station and he lifted her in his arms. The look of naked relief on her face finally clued him in as to what was going on with her. His pace quickened as he mounted the steps with her arms clamped tight around him. The contact fired through his whole body, adding to the sheer surrealism of the whole situation.

He kept her close, protecting her from the lunchtime throng as they made their way out of the station into the sunlight. When she tried to wriggle free, he held on.

'Which way?'

'Past the traffic lights and up the hill. My apartment is on the left,' she murmured.

He moved before she'd finished speaking, his stride long and purposeful, fuelled by a need so strong he felt every inch of skin suffused by it.

Obsession…

No, he was overreacting to a word that had no bearing on what was going on between him and Reiko.

Obsession had been his father and his grandfather's disease. It had been Isadora's.

He'd left every connotation of it behind in Arizona. The fact that it had popped into his head as he'd kissed Reiko meant nothing. It held no power over him if he didn't give it room. He sucked in a deep breath.

'Put me down, Damion. Your bodyguards are watching us. How did they get here so fast anyway?'

He kept on walking, his arms tightening around her. 'GPS

on my phone. They've been following us since we came out of the train station.'

The SUV rolled behind them as they strode up the hill.

'And they're going to be camped outside my apartment the whole time?'

'Unless you attack me with a butter knife. In which case I hit the alarm on my watch and they crash in commando-style.'

The smile he'd been looking for didn't materialise. In fact she grew paler the closer they got to her apartment. She knew the brevity of the next few hours.

So did he.

Her apartment was spacious, light and tastefully decorated. Eastern-influenced rugs decorated the wooden floors and Chinese and Japanese art graced the walls. A huge painting of a cherry-blossom tree took up almost one entire wall. One extra-large sofa dominated the room, behind which stood a very masculine-looking oak screen.

After dropping her bag on a nearby table, she hit a switch.

The opposite wall glowed yellow, then red. The next minute three fat orange holographic goldfish glided past.

He glanced at her. Despite her drawn features, a small smile curved her lips. 'You didn't believe me, did you?'

'I'm interested to see how the feeding part comes into it. It is, after all, the reason you ran away from me.'

She looked him square in the eye. 'I've stopped running.'

The jolt that went through his system threatened to knock him off his feet. When she turned away from him, Damion curbed the strong urge to pull her back. Instead he shoved his restless hands in his pockets and followed her into the kitchen.

'You're willing to open yourself up to me?'

She stiffened in the process of pulling open the fridge door. 'Let's not get ahead of ourselves, Baron. Like my lovely gold-fish out there, I'm an acquired taste. I'm pretty sure the minute you find out what's lurking underneath you'll run a mile.' A shadow of pain crossed her face.

His jaw tightened. 'You're making presumptions again, Reiko.'

Her small smile held even more pain. Somewhere in the region of his chest, a dull fire of anger took hold of him.

'We'll see. I can make us some lunch. Are you allergic to anything I should know about?' she asked.

'Only being prejudged. What happened on the train?'

Her fingers tightened around the bottle of *sake* she'd pulled out from the fridge.

'Don't you want something to eat?' she asked, her voice barely above a whisper.

'No.' Food was the last thing on his mind.

When she remained frozen where she stood, he opened cupboards until he located glasses. He took the bottle from her hand, poured and handed one glass to her.

The *sake* was the vilest he'd ever tasted, but he drank it anyway.

'The train, Reiko? What happened?'

She made a sound of distress, sagged against the sink and closed her eyes. 'My father… The crash two years ago… It happened on a train in Osaka.'

Reiko heard his sharp inhalation, felt the force of his fixed gaze upon her, knew the moment he strode forward and gasped as he lifted her into his arms. With quick strides he went into the living room.

When he deposited her at the end of the sofa, she finally opened her eyes. She saw him disappear into the kitchen and return with their drinks.

Her heart hammered as he took a seat next to her. She knew with every fibre of her being that once she told him he would leave and she'd most likely never see Damion again. The thought made her heart ache. Her gaze travelled over him, avidly keeping a record of the perfection of the man sitting a mere touch away.

'You're breaking the rules.' The edginess in his tone belied the lazy hand he lifted to take a sip of his drink.

'What rules?'

'Keeping our hands off each other until we've talked.'

'But…I haven't touched you!'

'*Ce n'est pas vrai.* Your eyes are touching me as surely as your hands yearn to. But first things first. If your father died in a train crash, why do you think it was your fault?'

Her breath caught. 'I…I forced him to go on the train. He didn't want to. I blackmailed him into it.'

'How?'

Reiko licked her lips, acute anxiety rolling through her at the thought of what she was about to reveal. 'I… He wanted me to…make some changes in my life. I wouldn't agree until he'd reconciled with my mother. They'd been separated for six months. He came to tell me he was going to divorce her. I didn't want him to.'

A pained look crossed his face. 'Not every marriage is destined to succeed. Sometimes walking away is the best option.'

'I know, but these were *my* parents. My mother isn't the most wifely or maternal of women, but even as flawed as she is I knew she wouldn't survive without my father. And in his own way he loved her. He agreed to give it one more try.'

'You were lucky. My parents stayed together and they died because of it.'

Shock rammed through her system. 'Oh, my God. How…? What happened?'

His gaze darkened until the grey was almost black. 'Obsession. They were cursed by their obsession.'

She stared back at him. 'What—?'

He waved her question away. 'We'll leave the sordid details of my childhood for another time. You were telling me what happened.'

Fighting the need to do something about his pain, she continued. 'I was living in Osaka when Dad came to see me. He hated taking trains, but I insisted because driving to Tokyo where my mother was would've taken longer.' The tight knot of pain that was never far away grew in her chest. 'Twenty minutes into the journey, the train crashed in a tunnel. We were trapped for two days. My father held my hand the whole time. By the time I finally got the courage to tell him I was sorry, he was dead. When my mother found out, she blamed me. Since my accident I've only seen her twice.'

She wasn't aware she was crying until Damion handed her a tissue. When he took her in his arms, the tears fell faster.

'Are your nightmares about the crash?'

She nodded against his chest. 'Sometimes I see him dying; sometimes I'm trapped in the twisted metal and I can't get to him. But it's always about the crash.'

'If your therapist was any good, she would've told you, despite what your mother thinks, your father's death isn't your fault.'

The warm note of sympathy in his voice made her tears flow faster.

'It doesn't matter what anyone says. I was selfish. I couldn't see beyond what I wanted. I didn't want to admit that maybe they were better off without each other. Dad loved her in his own way, but I know he was only seeking the reconciliation because of me—that given the choice he'd have divorced her. I also let him believe that my lifestyle choice was in some way his fault.'

'What lifestyle choice?'

Her heart lurched, then hammered. Reiko opened her mouth but couldn't find the strength to utter the words. Shame raked through her.

'What lifestyle choice?' he asked again.

The edge was back in his voice. When she glanced at him, she saw the rigid tension freezing his body.

She licked her lips. 'The partying…the men.'

Silence throbbed in the living room. His hand on the seat

tightened into a fist. 'How many were there?' he finally asked into the charged atmosphere.

'Damion—'

'How many?'

She named the figure. Damion's face turned ashen beneath his normally healthy tan. Before her very eyes she saw him recoil. His throat moved as he visibly swallowed.

And every second Reiko lived through the look in his eyes made her want to sink into the ground.

He surged to his feet. And without another word he walked out.

Reiko wasn't sure how long she remained frozen on the sofa. She knew it was a long time because her throat felt raw from crying and the living room was cloaked in darkness save for the intermittent glow from her goldfish.

Damion had left, just as she'd predicted. The small part of her that wasn't writhing in pain felt relieved. Really, she'd been saved from compounding his disgust with her by not letting him push her into revealing her outward scars. She couldn't have borne him recoiling from her scars the same way he'd recoiled from her other admissions.

She traced the scar on her face, fresh tears falling when she recalled Damion kissing it only a few days ago.

Pity. It had just been pity. Her fingers massaged her temple, and then she realised the pounding she could hear wasn't just in her head.

She dropped her hand, and her gaze flew to the door as the pounding grew louder.

'Reiko! Open the door,' came the firm command.

She stood and swayed with light-headedness. One shaky hand scrubbed across her face as the pounding came again.

Sniffing back more tears, she lit the nearest lamp and opened the door. 'What do you want, Damion?' she asked the imposing figure filling her doorway.

He stepped forward, shut the door behind him and held up a bottle of expensive red wine. 'That *sake* you served was an affront to my taste buds. I thought we'd need something more palatable.'

'You left…to buy wine?'

'This isn't just any wine, *ma belle*. It's a Bordeaux from my personal vineyard.'

His words were easy enough, but his gaze held a grim purpose that stopped her breath.

'Damion…'

'We haven't finished talking.' He went to the sofa and set the bottle down on the table unopened. 'Come and sit down, Reiko.'

'Why did you really leave?' she asked.

His lips firmed, and she thought he wouldn't answer. Then he shoved a hand through his hair. 'Most men don't like to think of a woman they've made love to making love with other men. In my case the thought makes me slightly insane.'

Surprise scythed through her. 'It does?'

His intense gaze rested on her. 'Remember what I said earlier about obsession?'

She nodded warily.

'My father suffered from obsessive behaviour, as did my grandfather when my grandmother was alive. On the train today, it struck me that I might be headed that way where you're concerned.'

She gasped. 'You *love* me?'

His laugh could have frozen water. 'Never confuse obsession with love, Reiko. Making that mistake made my childhood one no child should be put through.'

'What happened?'

'I was the pawn my father used to try to keep my mother in line. She was trapped in a marriage she didn't want, and he wouldn't give her a divorce because he thought she belonged to him. He eventually killed her and then took his own life.'

Her horrified gasp produced a grim smile.

'When I went to live with my grandparents, I fooled myself into thinking things would change. They didn't. My grandmother used me to cover her infidelities—I won't tell you the number of times I was late to school because she needed to see a *friend*—and my grandfather knew but was so besotted with her he forgave her. Each time it happened I saw him lose a piece of himself.'

'I saw you together at the exhibition. You seemed close.'

Damion lids lowered. 'There were times when my grandmother wasn't around that he seemed a different man. It made the nightmarish times easier to bear.'

Several pieces of the puzzle that was Damion fell into place. 'That's why you're trying to find the painting, even though you detest your grandmother?'

He picked up the bottle and started to remove the foil. 'His last wish is to be buried with the *Femme sur Plage*. I won't stand in the way of that wish.'

The finality of the statement told her it was time to move on. But she couldn't. She cleared her throat. 'So…you're becoming obsessed with me?'

His fingers stilled. 'I hope not, because that could be bad news for both of us.'

She licked suddenly dry lips. 'Wh…why?'

He looked up and speared her gaze with his. 'You've never asked me how I found out about that other man.'

She swallowed. 'How did you?'

His laugh was a harsh sound that echoed in the semi-darkness. 'I flew back two weeks after I left because I couldn't stop thinking about you. I tracked you down to your favourite wine bar in Tokyo. You were in a corner, kissing him. When you left, I followed you.' He shrugged at her gasp. 'When you took him to your apartment, I wanted to kill you both. That's when I knew I had to stay away.'

'And now?'

His gaze darkened. 'I can't bear the thought of you with other men, but to hate you for it would be hypocritical.'

'Damion…'

'Was it because of me? Did you sleep with him because I left you?' he grated out.

That was the one question she'd been dreading. To answer would be to reveal how much power he'd had over her. But she couldn't lie. 'Yes. I was devastated that you'd lied to me about who you were, then tried to pay me off like I was some sleazy mistake after my grandfather died. I hated you, but I think I hated myself more. It happened only once. I…I never saw him again.'

He cursed under his breath. '*Je suis désolé.* There were many times when I wanted to tell you, but each day that went by made it harder.' He shrugged. 'I guess I wanted you more than I wanted your forgiveness. I'm sorry, but I'm not perfect.'

The tight knot loosened inside her. 'I think we've established conclusively that neither of us are.'

He rounded the table and came towards her. 'I still want you.'

She backed away from him. 'Wait! I think there's something you should know.'

A fierce gleam lit his eyes. 'I don't want to hear about the men, Reiko.'

'That's just it. I went out with a lot of them, but after that first one I didn't sleep with any of them. I stupidly let my father think the worst of me so he'd stay with my mother.'

His eyes widened in surprise. His chest expanded on a heavy exhale. Then he renewed his pursuit. 'Reiko—'

She retreated. 'That doesn't mean I'll… You're… I can't sleep with you, Damion.'

His stride didn't break. 'Ah, *oui*, your little nugget about not being able to have sex. We still haven't discussed that bombshell.'

She shook her head. 'You don't want to hear it, Damion. It's not pretty.'

'Sex rarely is, *ma petite*,' he growled. Then he tried to reach for her again.

She backed away until her back touched the screen that had belonged to her father. 'Stop. I can't have you going all growly on me if you want this conversation to continue.'

He stopped and folded his arms, but his eyes, which had gone a dark, stormy grey, never left her face.

She licked her lips and the look in his eyes turned so forcefully primal her heart lurched.

'Seven months after the accident, my therapist thought it was time for me to stop hiding away, to try to make new friends, form new relationships. I gave it a try. I even went on…one date…'

His biceps flexed as his folded arms tightened. 'What happened?'

Pain racked through her as she recalled that night. 'It was messy. It was embarrassing—and…bloody. And it was one of the most painful experiences of my life. I really don't know why it happened. One moment everything was okay, the next my whole insides froze. I felt as if my body was physically rejecting him from the inside out. It…it was scary.'

Damion cursed, long and heavy, in French. When he jerked away from her, she was convinced this time when he left he wouldn't return. To her surprise, he went to the window. His silence was so complete, so humiliatingly deathly, Reiko was sure she could hear the dust motes falling to the floor.

He stood there for a long time; tension screamed from his body, so forbiddingly rigid her insides started to crumble.

'I told you you would be disgusted.' The pain straining through her made her voice emerge reed-thin and broken.

He whirled, a look of astonishment on his face. '*Disgusted?* Why would I be?'

'You're on the other side of the room, barely wanting to be

within sniffing distance of me. The dots are surprisingly easy
to connect.'

What happened next clarified the term *greased lightning*.

Because somehow she was in Damion Fortier's lap, her chin
held firmly in his grasp as he commanded her attention.

'I'm *not* disgusted. If you even *think* like that about yourself, I'll find those thumbscrews you've been hankering for
and take delight in applying them. *After* I've spent one night
proving you wrong.'

His arrogance made her blink. 'Wow—a whole night?' she
said snarkily.

He didn't take the bait. 'I'm thorough. You know that.'

The kiss he pressed against her lips was gentle, tear-jerking.

'Stop doing that!' She tried to wrench her chin from his
grasp but he held firm.

'What?'

'You're making me hate you less. And since I've spent the
last five years hating you, it feels…weird.'

'Weird as in escaped-from-a-zoo weird? Or helplessly-
attracted-to-you weird?'

'More of the former, less of the latter.'

His smile lifted the mood, easing the ache in the chest. 'I'm
thinking it's the other way round, *oui*?'

'*Oui—non!* You're confusing me, Baron. And that irritates
the hell out of me.'

She tried to get away from him. A strong hand clamped on
her waist. In the process of turning, she nudged the very real
force of his erection. Heat washed over her face. Her furtive
glance caught him still watching her, hawk-eyed. His smile
had widened.

'I confuse you. You turn me on. Right this moment every
bone in my body wants to prove it to you in a thousand different ways.'

'Because you're such a connoisseur of women?'

'Because the chemistry between us is as potent as ever. I

can't wait to see you naked again,' he breathed against her cheek.

And just like that every single atom in her being froze.

'Arrête!' he rasped against her jaw.

Reiko tensed even more. Frustration built inside him. Never in his life had getting through to someone been so difficult. And never in his life had he wanted to try with every fibre of his being.

He looked at her—the fight in her face, her desperation to hide her vulnerability—and something squeezed inside his chest. He forced himself to relax.

'Stop tensing. It's not good for your muscles. As for freezing me out—we've gone way past that.'

Her lips started to pout in annoyance. It took several deep breaths for him to resist the urge to taste her again. The time would come soon enough.

First he had more secrets to disclose. He took another breath.

'I met Isadora Baptiste soon after I left Tokyo.'

Tension gripped her harder. He ran his hand over her knee to clasp one warm, shapely calf and massaged gently until she started to relax.

'I'm not proud of it, but I tried to use her to forget you. It was only ever supposed to be temporary.'

Her lush lips firmed, and she wore a look of pained contempt. 'She was a married woman.'

'No, she wasn't. She'd been divorced for three years when I met her. But her fashion house was tied into her husband's business. Shares would've hit rock bottom if the public had found out she was no longer married to Antoine Baptiste.'

'So it was better to be branded an adulteress in the interests of a healthy share price?'

'Don't sneer. Empires and dynasties have risen and fallen on the right marriage alliances. It's as real in the twenty-first century as it was in the first.'

'What about her children? Did she really abandon them?'

Damion's insides clamped painfully. His guilt at knowing he'd unwittingly exacerbated the situation pierced sharply as much now as it had when he'd found out.

'*Oui*, that is true.'

Her face reflected anger and disappointment. His heart raced with the need to obliterate both emotions.

'Three months after I met her, she asked me to meet her children. I didn't think I was equipped to be any sort of influence on children. I refused. She took it to mean I didn't like children. I didn't realise she'd cut them out of her life until her ex-husband informed me.' Remembering what else Isadora had done, he felt his insides congeal with the familiar mix of pity and anger. 'It turned out she wasn't quite stable.'

Her eyes darted to his face and stayed. Slowly a breath eased out of her. 'Why did you break up with her?'

'Because I realised too late she epitomised everything I was trying to turn my back on.'

'She was obsessed with you?'

He nodded. 'After her husband told me she'd cut her children out of her life, I confronted her. It didn't go well. Two hours later I found her in the bath, with her wrists slashed.'

CHAPTER TEN

'MY GOD!' SHOCK WAVES vibrated through her as she stared at Damion. The gleam of pain she'd seen in his eyes intensified. Against every need for self-preservation, she placed her hand on his hard cheek. 'That can't have been easy.'

'It wasn't,' he stated baldly. 'It became clear very quickly she had a serious problem. It was the reason Antoine had divorced her. I found her a facility in Arizona and arranged for her to be taken in.'

She remembered their conversation in the restaurant in Paris. 'You went with her?'

He nodded. 'I stayed for the first few weeks—until it became clear it wasn't a *what* that was triggering her condition. It was *who*.'

A bleak look entered his eyes that tore at her insides. 'You?'

He took her hand from her cheek and planted a soft kiss in her palm. Deep inside, Reiko felt something give—something she tried to gather back into solid form but failed.

'So far I haven't found a way to forgive myself for what I put her through. I knew the signs of obsession, yet I completely missed them. It won't happen again.'

He looked directly into her eyes, and the raw vulnerability in his gaze stopped her breath.

'Damion—'

'I've laid myself bare to you, *ma fleur*. I have no regrets for doing so because I want you to trust me. With everything.'

Her heart lurched. 'I…I can't. It's too painful.'

Fully expecting an argument, she was extremely surprised when he nodded and kissed her forehead. 'It is a daunting process. I understand. But we will get there.'

We.

That simple word scared her more than the hardened determination oozing from his every pore.

Long fingers drifted up her thigh, over her skirt to the silk shirt. Desire shoved the pain aside, escalating the deep melting inside her. When his lips drifted down from her forehead to her cheek, and finally to her lips, Reiko sighed with the pleasure that stole through her.

Until she felt him release the first of her buttons. 'What are you doing?'

'What I've been dying to do since I saw you through Ashton's window last week.'

His heated gaze fell to her exposed throat and drifted down to the cleavage he was in the process of exposing. Another button popped open.

She squeaked and tried to sidle away from him. He stilled her with very little effort.

'I want to see you, Reiko.' Fierce determination deepened his voice.

The threat of exposure made ice dance down her spine. 'I...I'm not ready for that.' Nor would she ever be ready. Humiliation would always win. She was scarred, both outside and inside. 'Besides, aren't you forgetting something, Damion?'

'What?'

'You're supposed to be finding a suitable bride—someone who will help seed the next Fortier generation.' Pain stabbed right through her, lingering in the empty womb where no child would ever grow.

Damion's gaze dimmed. 'That will happen eventually. First I must do this.'

'Why? Why *must* you?'

'I hurt you. I know that now. Give me the chance to make reparations.'

'By sleeping with me again? Can't I just say I forgive you?'

Damion shook his head. 'You think there's something wrong

with you. I want to prove to you there isn't. Don't worry, *ma belle*, we'll take it slow.'

Another button popped open and Reiko wondered why in hell's name she wasn't screaming in terror.

Intrigued despite herself, she watched his face. 'What does taking it slow mean?'

He smiled. 'For now, I just want to open your shirt.'

'Nothing more?' she asked.

'That's entirely up to you.'

With the last of the buttons freed, he gently parted the lapels, his gaze on her face the whole time. When his hand slid over the waistband of her skirt and touched her midriff, every nerve-ending in her body screamed with pleasure.

'What do *you* want, Reiko?'

Her gaze dropped to his lips. 'For you to kiss me—'

He sealed his mouth over hers before she'd finished the sentence. Pleasure exploded underneath her skin and very quickly threatened to slide out of control. Her nipples peaked against the satin bra. Beneath her, the force of his erection probed forcefully against her bottom.

A small part of her wept at the thought that she'd never experience what it was like to make love with Damion again. The greedy part of her took what she could.

Her fingers sank into his hair and she revelled in his groan as his arms tightened around her. Heat pooled low in her belly, a demanding throb starting between her legs that made her clamp her thighs together.

Nothing could come of this. Nothing…

When Damion's hand clamped over her bottom and squeezed, Reiko gasped, a shudder raking through her frame.

He paused and slowly raised his head. 'Enough?'

Every instinct screamed *no*. But she knew there was only one answer she could give. Pushing away the sharp stab of pain, she swallowed. 'Enough.'

* * *

Damion called the dealer who'd bought the *Femme sur Plage* the next morning and offered him a price he couldn't refuse.

By noon the painting had been returned. Three hours later, they were on their way to the airport.

In his hurry to get moving, Damion hadn't bothered to wrap the painting. As the sleek, luxurious private jet took off and winged its way back to France, Reiko gazed at the painting leaning against the cabin wall, wondering how a woman so staggeringly beautiful could have been the way Damion had described her.

'What are you going to do with the other paintings?'

A myriad emotions criss-crossed Damion's face before it froze into the carefully neutral mask he adopted so well. 'I've thought of burning them a few times—'

'You wouldn't dare!'

'But I guess my children deserve to know what a messed-up family they're born into.'

The mention of children sent a horrid vein of chill through her. For two years she'd swept the issue of children blithely under her mental carpet—*out of sight, out of mind.*

Now she reeled under the impact of a thousand mental pictures of Damion's children and fought to catch her breath.

Across from her, Damion frowned. 'What's wrong? You've gone pale.'

She glanced down at her hands. 'Guess I'm still jet lagged. I barely managed to get rid of the last bout before jumping on a plane again.'

He studied her for several seconds, during which she held her breath, afraid a single movement would crack her open and expose all her secrets.

When his gaze moved back to the painting, his thoughts obviously still occupied by haunting memories of his childhood, Reiko heaved a sigh of relief.

A shadow crossed his face. 'I guess you must think me heartless for the way I feel towards my family?'

She shook her head, tensing when his gaze traced the scar she'd unwittingly revealed. Reiko itched to cover it. Instead she took a deep breath and reached for his hand. Warm fingers curled into hers, his eyes darkening as he glanced down at their entwined fingers.

'No. I suspected that a family as outwardly pristine as yours would be hiding epically gruesome skeletons. But I'd like you to stop pretending you're not upset by all of this,' she murmured, with an ache in her heart for what he'd suffered.

'A lifetime of witnessing volatile emotions on a daily basis either teaches you to replicate the same behaviour or bury it.'

'You're talking about obsession. What about love?'

He shrugged. 'I've survived this far with the barest minimum. It doesn't feature high on the list of things I crave.'

A band of discomfort tightened around her chest. 'So you feel no remorse for all the broken hearts you've scattered around Europe?'

He raised their entwined hands and brushed feather-light kisses on her knuckles. 'A prince has to kiss a lot of girl-frogs to find the right match.'

His gaze settled on her, and an inscrutable gleam in his eyes caused alarm to skitter across her skin.

'But I think my search is almost over.'

His tone had lightened, his face unfreezing from the icy mask it had been minutes ago. But almost in direct proportion, Reiko felt her insides clamp down hard with the echo of his words.

She had no part in that scenario. Just as she had no right to feel that the ache in her heart was the most painful thing she'd ever experienced.

Château Fortier, the centuries-old ancestral seat of the Fortiers, was soaked in rain as their car approached along the tree-lined, double-width lane. Reiko gaped in wonder at the dark waters lapping the stone walls.

There was a genuine moat. And an honest-to-goodness drawbridge.

She tried to suppress the hysterical bubble of amusement that rose in her throat. She succeeded. Only to lose it at the first sight of the *château*.

Beside her, in the back seat of the silver limousine that had transported them from the private airport in Bordeaux, she felt Damion's keen gaze swing her way.

The car stopped at the end of the sweeping driveway. She looked up at the never-ending fairytale splendour of Château Fortier and shook her head. 'He never stood a chance.'

'Who didn't?'

She heard the frown in his voice. 'My grandfather. Against all this.' She indicated with the wave of her hand. 'Your grandfather had this; mine was just a poor art student from a suburb of Kyoto on scholarship to the Sorbonne when he met your grandmother. There was no way he could offer her anything like this.'

Damion's frown was replaced by a carefully neutral look, but not before she spotted the hint of regret in his eyes.

'Money isn't everything,' he dismissed.

Reiko blew out an exasperated breath through the sadness welling up inside her. 'That's rubbish. Only the people with money tend to trot out that piece of nonsense. Money buys power. Power is a drug few people can resist.'

'*You've* set aside the pursuit of it for a higher purpose.'

'We're not talking about me. We're talking about how mean life can be sometimes.'

His eyes narrowed as he slammed the boot and came to stand before her. Tilting her chin with one long, slim finger, he let his gaze rake her face. 'But if you could have anything you want, what would you choose, Reiko?'

For you not to have walked away.

For me not to be left with emotional and physical scars because of my mistakes.

She couldn't even think about the third and deepest wish, so she looked away from him and started counting the turrets that graced the *château*. When she ran out of fingers to count on, she sucked in a composing breath and glanced back at him.

'For now? A tour would be nice. Maybe a cheese panini thrown in at the end? I'm starving. You think your chef can rustle one up for me if I ask nicely?'

'Without question.' He took her arm and led her through the double-pillared entrance into the *château*. 'But first we'll do your exercises.'

Her pulse shot into overdrive. 'What do you mean, *we*? I can do them on my own.'

'You're in pain again. Don't try to tell me otherwise. As much as your exaggerated walk is sexy as hell, I can't overlook the reason behind it. So—exercise first, then the tour, before food.'

'Did anyone tell you you're an insufferable tyrant?'

His jaw tightened. 'No, but I understand some think I'm a stuffy Frenchman. Tell me—if I pick you up will I hurt you?'

She felt her resolve weakening, an ever-growing need to set down the chafing reins of self-control. Just to let go…for a little while. 'No, but why—?'

He swung her up into his arms, held her close to his chest and mounted the stone steps that led into the *château*.

Over his shoulder she could see beautifully landscaped gardens stretch as far as the eye could see, above her she caught a view of a slate-roofed turret, and the feeling of being overwhelmed washed over her again. There was just so much—of the man, of his wealth and prestige, of the history in this place.

She looked at his profile and felt an overwhelming need to touch his face. Giving in to it, she traced her fingers over his jaw. Hard, warm, slightly rough. And so evocatively sexy she couldn't resist leaning up to press her lips against his skin.

He stumbled to a halt in the hallway. Above the din of blood roaring through her ears, she heard him dismiss the driver and the housekeeper. He stared down at her, the look in his eyes so captivating and powerful she trembled.

'See how far we've come, *ma petite*? Now you kiss me because to resist is simply too painful. And you touch me because you want to. Not because you want to gain the upper hand.'

Surprise shot through her, making her drop her hand. 'You knew?'

He smiled and brought his nose down to nuzzle hers. 'It's an effective tool. I've always found it difficult to think straight when your hands are on me.'

Heat seared through her belly and flooded her whole being until she felt engulfed by it. When his lips lowered an extra half-inch to capture hers in a blistering kiss, she gave in to a desire that left her gasping for breath afterwards.

By the time he lifted his head, her senses were swimming. She closed her eyes for several seconds to regain her equilibrium. When she finally opened them, he was striding towards the right wing of a spectacular sweeping staircase.

Finally looking around, Reiko caught her first glimpse of the interior of Château Fortier.

Thick walls were decorated with portraits of past Fortiers, interspersed with stunning pieces of art and antiquities. Masterpieces dotted the hallway, and at the base of each staircase two French marble busts stood in complete prominence.

He made it to the top of the stairs and turned down the east corridor. Antique leather trunks dotted the hallway, and above her exquisitely cut crystal chandeliers set into vaulted ceilings gleamed and sparkled.

The suite Damion entered was the last word in luxury. The blue-and-gold décor was impossibly beautiful and followed the magnificently warm yet stunningly extravagant theme of Château Fortier. A huge sleigh bed stood on a dias, and had an honest-to-goodness intricately designed canopy that fed an endless curtain of white muslin around the bed.

Her gasp of appreciation drew Damion's attention. 'You like it?' he asked.

'What's not to like? It's completely breathtaking. I'm almost too scared to touch anything in case I break it.'

He set her down, but kept his arms around her. 'Objects can be replaced. Your comfort is what's important.' He leaned down and kissed her forehead. 'But if you get too scared, feel free to knock on my door. I'm right through there.' He nodded towards a connecting door on the far side of the room.

The sensation that shot through her had nothing to with the stiffness in her body and everything to do with the way this man made her feel on a constant basis.

The knowledge that he was stepping up his campaign to get her into his bed should have frightened her, but all Reiko felt was an inferno-like desire raging through her, loosening the notch on her control a little more.

Would it hurt just to take this one last opportunity to be with him?

Yes!

Desperately, she tried to scramble back control. 'That probably won't be necessary. I don't spook that easily.'

He pulled her close until her breasts touched his chest. Her nipples peaked and by the catch in his breath she knew he'd felt them.

'I'd advise you to keep the door locked, then. I may not be able to help myself.' He took her mouth again, this time deepening the kiss with a bold stroke of his tongue.

Reiko whimpered as desire scoured through her. At the back of her mind she called herself ten kinds of fool for giving in to this dangerously heady situation. But when it came to Damion her willpower had always been pathetically deficient.

By the time he stepped back and sucked in a deep breath,

she was ready to throw caution to the wind, consequences be damned.

The dark stamp of desire on his face told its own lust-ramping story. 'I need to get out of here. Tell me to get out of here, Reiko.'

She licked tingling lips, fighting the need to say the opposite. 'Get out of here, Damion.'

He gave a harsh sigh, took another step back and thrust his fingers through his hair. 'Get your swimsuit and meet me downstairs in five minutes.'

'Where are we going?'

An enigmatic smile crossed his lips. 'I have a surprise for you.' His gaze dropped to her feet. 'And wear sensible shoes.' With that, he turned and left the room.

For several seconds, she remained where she stood, her senses crashing like an addict on a downward spiral. Damion seemed to have taken the very air and vitality of life with him, leaving her craving and desperate.

Catching herself standing there like a lovelorn fairytale maiden, she forced herself to move. But as she caught a glimpse of a gilt-edged, intricately designed mirror she knew was from the boudoir of a French empress, she couldn't help but feel that she *was* in a fairytale. Every ornament, rug and painting was embroidered in the rich tapestry of history. History that would be here long after she had passed through.

Long after Damion had installed his chosen wife in the *château* and sired countless babies and she was but a distant memory.

Pain roused her from her lethargy. Firming her lips, she moved past the bed towards a door she rightly guessed to be the dressing room.

Her suitcase had arrived in her room before she had—a testament to just how efficiently everything moved in Damion's world..

She found the Lycra unitard she'd used in Paris and quickly

slipped it on. Feeling adequately covered, she slipped her feet into a pair of ballerina pumps and made her way downstairs.

She caught Damion's frown long before she descended the gloriously curved staircase.

'That is not a swimsuit,' he rasped, displeasure in his voice.

'Sorry to disappoint. If you expect me to parade in front of you in a skimpy number, it's not going to happen. I don't own a swimsuit.' She'd burned them all in a dark haze a month after the accident. And she didn't regret the decision.

'I can—'

'No. I'm sure you have a whole wardrobe full of bikinis tucked away somewhere in this vast place, but I'll pass, thanks. This is an all-purpose outfit. It'll do for whatever it is you have in mind.'

His gaze drifted over her and Reiko found out very quickly that the tungsten-laced outfit was no match for the heated intensity in Damion's eyes. Feeling her nipples peak and heat pool between her legs again, she shifted restlessly.

'Damion…'

'*Alors*, let's go,' he commanded, his voice deeply husky.

He took her hand and led her behind the left staircase. They descended several steps and ended up in front of a large black-painted door.

'You're taking me to the dungeon?'

His smile held a wealth of dark promise. 'Not just yet.'

The door opened into a small but well-lit hallway. Limestone walls and grey floor slates echoed the sound of their passage as he led her deeper underneath the *château*.

After several twists and turns, they passed underneath a stone arch and emerged into an enclosed space. At first she didn't see it because she was too captivated by the sight of Damion's broad shoulders. When she managed to prise her gaze away, Reiko gasped at the stunning sight before her.

The pool was surrounded on three sides by hanging foliage and lit underneath so the water glowed a soft, mesmerising aqua. The faint rush of water reached her ears, and she turned left to see a small inlet from where the pool flowed. Next to it stood a large wooden bench and a stone table that held a stack of towels.

The place was simply…perfect.

'Ready?'

Damion had stripped to swimming trunks. What little breath she'd retained immediately evaporated. At her jerky nod, he took her hand and led her down the shallow stone slabs into the water.

'It's warm!'

'It's a thermal pool that flows from the mountain. It isn't always warm. I had special heating rods placed in so it stays warm all year round.'

He pulled her to him and turned her round, so her back was tucked against his front. He leaned against the side and trailed his lips over her ear. Despite the renewed charge of desire, Reiko could already feel the healing powers of the water working wonders on her body. Relaxing further into him, she sighed with pleasure.

'Thank you for this. It's just perfect.'

He kissed her jaw. 'You're welcome. But you still have work to do. Put your arms around my neck.'

She reached back and linked her arms behind his neck. Her exposed position stirred the beginnings of vulnerability. She wasn't foolish enough to dismiss the sexual power Damion had over her. With a single touch he could make her shed all common sense and more. Already her breasts had grown heavy, and her breath snagged in her chest as his hands drifted down over her thighs.

But he was all business. He reached down and pulled her knees up to her chest. Immediately the muscles in her back stretched and started to release their tightness. Slowly he repeated the movement, taking instruction from her and expertly putting her through her paces.

After almost forty-five minutes, she performed her last stretch. He turned her around in his arms.

'Are you okay?' His face held concern.

She smiled. 'Don't worry. I'm not going to shed tears all over you.'

'*Bien sûr.* That is good to know. And before you say it, *oui*, I'm agitated.'

He pulled her closer. The evidence of his arousal made a bubble of laughter burst free.

'You think this is funny?'

'Maybe. But it's definitely sexy.'

His answer was a deep growl as he hauled her out of the water. With quick, sure strides, he approached the bench and laid her on it. He came down on top of her before she could draw breath.

Damion's kiss was fervent to the point of desperation. He kissed her as if he wanted to devour her whole, his hands urgent on her body. When he captured one breast in his hand, she cried out with the pleasure of it. The sound only inflamed him further.

He muttered dark, throaty words as he settled himself between her legs and recaptured her lips, plunging his tongue into her mouth with a bold stake-claiming move that sent her closer to the edge.

Demanding hands trailed over her body. He lowered the zipper of the suit and captured one nipple in his mouth.

Fire exploded through her, scorching her from head to toe in blissful desire. He tugged, teased, sucked and licked before turning his attention to the twin breast.

Finally he shifted to caress one hand over her stomach. Her newly relaxed muscles immediately clenched. When his hand moved lower and settled between her thighs, she held her breath, feelings of fearful insecurity rising to mingle with desire.

'It's okay. Trust me,' he murmured.

In slow, steady movements, he pressed his hand between her legs and caressed her through the wetsuit. Her head went back, her body arching of its own accord into the powerful play of his hand. Liquid heat oozed through her legs, her clitoris swelling as Damion found and played with the nerve-engorged nub.

His head descended and his tongue circled one nipple. She cried out at the double sensation, her heart hammering with enough force to make her breaths gush. With an expertly timed sequence, he licked and rubbed, pushing her closer and closer to the edge, all the while murmuring hot, decadent words to her in French.

Her fingers plunged into his hair, desperately searching for an anchor in the storm of bliss battering her. He showed no mercy. With one final flick of his fingers and a long pull on her nipple, he sent her surging into the stars.

Reiko was dimly aware of thrashing beneath him, of crying out hoarsely as wave after endless wave of pleasure rolled over her. She even felt him zip up her suit and trail kisses over her face, catch the lone tear that rolled from one eye. But she couldn't find the words or the strength to do anything but soak in the moment.

She'd fallen apart, lost control completely…and there'd been no pain, no humiliation. She opened her eyes.

Was Damion right? Was there really nothing wrong with her? The thought of how it would feel to have him touch her, *really* touch her, sent a wave of renewed heat through her…

Until the realisation that she was contemplating making love again with Damion Fortier sent a cold shockwave through her.

But would it be so wrong? He's already seen your scars.

But he hadn't seen the worst of them. And once he did…

'For a woman who's just climaxed in my arms, you're thinking far too hard for my liking.'

She looked at him. The harsh stamp of desire on his face had deepened, as if giving her satisfaction had fuelled his own needs. Against her stomach, the unabated evidence nudged her. She nudged back.

His heavy groan echoed over the water. With a deep sigh,

he levered himself away from her. She felt bereft at the loss of his warmth and heavy weight.

'Where are you going?'

He stood and gazed down at her. 'You're not ready, and I refuse to resort to wet humping.'

Excitement loosened her tongue. 'I don't know—it has its benefits.'

'I fail to see what they are.'

Her smile was decidedly impish. 'For a start, there's no chafing.'

Despite the dangerous heat in his eyes, he laughed.

The sound curled inside her, sparking a different set of flames she refused to examine closely. Leaning down, he placed an open-mouthed kiss just above her belly button.

'*C'est vrai*, I'm saved from chafing.'

He straightened and headed for the shower. Watching him go, she swallowed against the forceful feelings roiling through her.

Damion Fortier was still the dangerous and frighteningly ruthless man she'd discovered five years ago. But in the past couple of days, he'd shown her a side of him she hadn't really seen before. He'd shown her he could be kind, supportive and incredibly generous.

His ruthless streak wasn't far from the surface, but these newly discovered traits of his character, coupled with his dangerously intent single-minded determination to go after what he wanted, were…sexy.

As for his body…

With the trunks moulded to his rear, she couldn't miss the hard, mouth-watering shape of it. Or the V-shaped torso that could easily have belonged to a Roman gladiator. Moisture gathered in her mouth and in other places as she kept staring at his back.

He moved beneath the first of the triple showers lining one side of the pool. At his deep shudder she guessed the temperature of the water was nowhere near the cosy temperature of the thermal pool.

Reiko swallowed, started to contemplate the wisdom of what she was thinking…and then stopped thinking altogether.

He tensed at the first touch of her hand. She gasped at how cold the water was.

Sluicing water out of his eyes, Damion whipped his head towards her. 'What are you doing?'

Her gaze fell to the still very much powerful erection, which hadn't abated despite the freezing cold.

'I was thinking I could…you know…help you out.' She licked her lips and his eyes gleamed dangerously.

'Five years ago you couldn't say *blow job* without blushing. That fact that you still can't makes me think you shouldn't be offering, *cherie.*'

She reddened even while her chin rose. 'Is that a dare?'

He braced one hand against the shower wall, his jaw tightening as he shut his eyes for one split second. 'It's a plea to get off this subject.'

Devilish delight danced through her. 'Why? Is it too *hard* for you?'

The sound he emitted was half groan, half stunned disbelief. 'Dammit, Reiko, don't push a desperate man to his limit.'

'But I'm offering the perfect solution.'

His hands lowered, his eyes turning the darker shade of grey she equated with Serious Damion.

'The next time I seek release with you, I want to be inside you. Nothing else will do.'

Pain ripped through her, the knowledge that that would never happen forcing a heavy, immovable lump into her chest. 'And if that never happens?'

'It will.'

He said it with such unshakeable certainly Reiko allowed herself to believe for a second. For one foolish, desperate second. Then reality crashed through.

As if he could guess her thoughts, an implacable expression settled on his face. 'Whatever you think is wrong with you, we'll overcome it. I'll accept nothing but success. And neither should you.'

'That's not what—'

He placed a long forefinger over her lips. 'We will make love, you and I. And you will cry out with the power of your release in my arms.' He stepped closer. 'For now, though, I'll take a kiss.'

'Is that wise?' she ventured.

'No, but that's what cold showers are for.'

'It doesn't seem to be working.' Boldly she let her gaze drop below his waist. 'If you don't have any other solution besides turning yourself into an ice sculpture, my offer still stands.'

'That's enough!' He snapped shut the water with enough force to break the faucet. Luckily, the cast-iron had no doubt withstood the force of the Fortier ire before. 'You're right. This isn't working.'

He snagged two towels and handed her one. Briskly he dried himself, then snapped a fresh towel around his waist. 'You still want a tour of the *château*?'

Bemused, she nodded.

His smile was grim. '*Bien sûr.* We'll start with the dungeons. There's a perfectly cosy male girdle there I suspect I'll need.'

Her stunned laugh only made his smile grimmer as he all but frogmarched her back to her suite.

CHAPTER ELEVEN

BEING NOBLE SUCKED.

Damion gritted his teeth as he took another cold shower at dawn.

His body had attained a life of its own. It craved Reiko Kagawa, and nothing, not even the punishing effects of the treadmill he'd pounded for the past two hours, eased the need.

Standing under sharp needles of freezing water was the only solution.

Not the only solution.

No. He couldn't take the path he so desperately wanted to. Reiko needed time.

It didn't take a genius to work out that her accident had affected her more than just physically. It wasn't surprising that she flinched every time he went too far with her.

His time in Arizona with Isadora had taught him the complexity of the human psyche. He'd returned with a grudging understanding of what had made his father and grandfather react the way they had. And it had made him even more determined never to fall into the same trap.

Isadora's self-esteem had been battered by one failed relationship by the time he'd met her. His confronting her about her failure as a mother had sent her over the edge.

If he pushed too hard with Reiko, she'd bolt. His body tensed in rejection of that idea. Standing under the freezing water, it occurred to Damion that this needn't be the case. There were other, *less* traumatising ways of bedding a woman.

He shoved a hand through his soaking hair.

That was just it. Every woman he could think of suddenly appeared...*less*.

The memory of Reiko exploding in his arms replayed in

his mind. His body immediately reacted, like to the pull of a siren's song.

With a stiff curse, he wrenched the tap shut. It was no use trying to unwrap the enigma of why he wanted Reiko. Five years ago his lust had had no rhyme or reason. It certainly didn't now, and he was damned if he would spend another moment freezing his balls off trying to wrestle meaning into why he felt the way he did.

Surely once he'd bedded her she'd lose her allure?

Returning to his bedroom, he squashed the mocking voice that told him he shouldn't be so sure.

'So what exactly is this job you have in mind for me?' Reiko asked Damion over breakfast.

'We'll get to that in a moment. How did you sleep?' he asked, his eyes raking her face in a frank, intimate scrutiny that immediately threw her back to last night and what had happened between them at the pool.

Heat rushed into her face. 'You can't do that!'

One brow shot up. 'I can't ask you how you slept?'

'You're looking at me *knowingly.*'

'That is because I've *known* you, *ma fleur.*'

She blew an exasperated breath and tried to keep her leaping pulse under control. Truth be told, she'd woken this morning to the sound of trilling birds, bright sunshine and the sinking feeling that keeping Damion at arm's length would prove harder than she'd imagined.

Even the thought of him seeing her, seeing her body so different from the one he'd known in the past, hadn't filled her with as much horror as she'd imagined it would.

She swallowed. 'I slept soundly. You?'

He set his cup down, picked up a fork and speared a plump, perfectly cut peach. 'I won't bore you with the intimate details of my restless night, *mon amour.* Let's just say my shower has been well exercised.' He held out the fruit to her.

Feeling another wave of heat wash through her, she opened her mouth and took the offering. His gaze dropped to her lips, and his grey eyes darkened to almost black.

'I won't feel guilty just because I slept better than you did.'

He smiled. 'On the contrary. I'm glad you did. You'll need your strength for when the time comes.'

'You're so sure you'll succeed, aren't you?'

'Oui,' he stated simply, with irritating assurance.

'Saru mo ki kara ochiru.' She couldn't help the need to pierce that arrogance.

His deep laugh struck a chord deep inside her, and before she knew it a smile broke over her face. He held another piece of fruit against her lips.

She accepted it, deliberately keeping her mouth wrapped around the fork for longer than was necessary. His breath hissed through his teeth.

'You're right. Even monkeys fall from trees,' he responded in a serious, deep tone. 'But I get the feeling this won't be one of those times. You want to be mine again as much as I want to be yours.'

The bold statement sobered her up. There was no way in a thousand years she and Damion would ever work. And no amount of arrogance on his part would make the reality of her condition any less palatable.

She was everything Damion Fortier would never accept in his perfect existence.

Desperately forcing aside the wave of despair that threatened to wash over her, she brushed a few crumbs from the table. 'You were about to tell me what my job entails.'

He frowned at her brisk tone and change of subject, but she breathed a sigh of relief when he set his fork down and nodded.

'For the first two weeks of every March, we open parts of the *château* to the public. During that time all the museums and galleries that hold Fortier art and paintings on loan are required to return them for exhibition. I'll provide you with a list, and you'll liaise with the various houses to co-ordinate the shipping and safe delivery of the pieces. I also have six pieces arriving from Kazakhstan tomorrow. Once you've examined them, I'll decide which ones to include in the exhibition.'

'Damn, I should have asked for double what you're paying me.'

He smiled. 'That's not all. There's also a ball at the end of the two weeks. I usually stage a show of the Fortier jewellery collection. You'll help organise that, too.'

She frowned. 'Don't you have a curator-slash-party-planner-type person for this sort of thing? Organising shows isn't really my thing.'

Darkness clouded his eyes. 'This will be my grandfather's last ball, so I want it to be special. He arrives tomorrow, by the way. Besides, the person I used last year is no longer available and I haven't found a replacement.'

His first statement made her insides soften with sympathy. His last hardened the softness immediately. 'You mean you dumped her.' It wasn't a question. 'I take it she was one of the girl-frogs who didn't quite make the cut?'

'What can I say? I'm a perfectionist.'

His words punched a hole through her. Pushing back her chair, she surged to her feet. 'Then what the hell are you doing with *me*? I'm very far from perfect.'

He caught her wrist and pulled her to him before she could escape. Swinging his legs from under the table, he rested both hands on her hips, trapping her between his legs. 'You're also a little damaged, wilful and, prone to defensive anger and bad language.'

'Who do you think you are? Freud?'

'I fully intend to cure you of all that.'

'*Cure me?* What? I'm like some pet project to you?'

'You're a very beautiful woman over whom I've spent several sleepless nights sporting a raging hard-on to end all hard-ons. My intentions aren't altogether altruistic, so don't make me out to be some sort of saint.'

She snorted despite her pain. 'Sainthood is the last honour I'd bestow on you.'

'Your trust is all I need, *ma fleur*.'

Another surge of despair deflated her hurt and anger. 'You ask for the impossible, Damion.'

His gaze darkened. *'Koketsu ni irazunba koji wo ezu.'* Nothing ventured, nothing gained.

And for the next week, Damion showed her just now determined he could be. And how utterly *he* was prepared to trust *her*. Reiko used her connections to speed up the delivery of pieces of art that were coming in from far-flung places such as Nicaragua and Zanzibar. The pieces from Kazakhstan arrived. Five of them were above board. She phoned through her suspicions over the last piece to Yoshi, then concentrated her efforts on the *château* opening.

With the help of the St Valoire committee, specially selected to assist with organising the open days and the ball, she watched with growing satisfaction as the *château* was transformed from stunning private residence to magnificent public masterpiece.

She was placing the last stack of glossy leaflets that gave a brief but rich history of the *château* on a Louis XIV credenza when strong arms slid around her waist.

'It's nearly seven. You were officially off the clock almost two hours ago.' Damion's lips teased the shell of her ear as he pulled her back against his warmth.

'I've never been a nine-to-five sort of girl,' she replied. Unable to resist, she leaned into him and felt his hardness against her backside.

All week he'd made such intimate gestures, sometimes in full view of his grandfather and the assistants running around trying to get the *château* ready. This morning their kiss had got so heated a committee member had coughed several times before they'd sprung apart.

And with every touch, every kiss, she felt her resistance eroding just a little further. Even now, resisting the urge to turn and bask in his magnificence, she knew it was only a matter of time before she gave in.

'As the boss, I'm calling it a day. And take those shoes off.' She heard the frown in his voice. 'I don't understand how you keep walking in those things.'

She finally turned to face him, fully prepared for the punch to her system the sight of his gorgeous face and incredible body always produced. 'I feel fine. The pool has worked wonders for my back…' Her words spluttered to a halt when he let go of her and knelt at her feet.

'It's still not a reason to abuse your health.' He grasped her calf. 'Off.'

Reiko grabbed the credenza to steady herself against the strange new emotion that battered her. The unexpected sight of Damion at her feet knocked the breath clean out of her lungs. There was nothing especially erotic or lustful about the gesture, but her senses screeched all the same, her heart hammering a beat so wild she almost gasped with the force of it.

'There—that's better.'

Disrobing her feet of the platform heels, he flung them to one side and surged up to tower over her. Without the benefit of her heels, he loomed bigger, larger than life, and he made her feel as delicate as cherry blossom as he gathered her into his arms.

'Damion…'

'I've been dying to kiss you properly since we were interrupted this morning.'

'I think we scandalised Madame LeBoeuf.'

'She needs to learn that discretion is the better part of valour,' he said huskily before he lifted her into his arms. 'Put your legs around me.'

She gasped at the image that shot into her mind. The intimacy of their position made the blood roar through her veins. He walked forward as he kissed her, taking his time to explore her mouth with an ease and expertise that left her reeling. She didn't know where he was taking her until a cool breeze touched her skin.

They were on the east side of the *château*, where an elevated terrace gave fantastic views over the valley. St Valoire was breathtaking during the day and mesmerising at night.

He set her down and she turned to find a single round table set out between two imposing arch-supporting columns. After seeing her seated, he lifted the lids off the plates.

A simple meal of *châteaubriand* with potato cutlets and green beans was accompanied by a rich, full-bodied Bordeaux from the *château*'s vineyard. After their meal was cleared away, they lingered over the last of the wine.

'Thanks for giving me this job. I wasn't sure I could pull it off, but I've had a blast.'

'You love art and you love a challenge. The combination was always going to work in your favour, and ultimately in mine.'

'But as you said it's your grandfather's last ball. You could've trusted a dozen other people with it. You trusted me. So thank you.'

He looked at her for a long time, an indecipherable expression entering his eyes before he lowered his lids.

The soft glow from the wall-ensconced lights threw shadows over his face as he leaned over to refill her crystal glass. She traced the chiselled perfection of his bone structure and the mouth that had kissed her senseless a short time ago.

He raised his gaze and caught hers. 'What?'

'You truly are spectacularly gorgeous, Damion.'

The wine bottle hit the table with a little more force than was necessary. 'Reiko…'

For the first time since she'd met him, he seemed at a loss for words. With widening eyes, she watched a flush creep over his taut cheeks.

She laughed. 'Oh, my God, I didn't mean to embarrass you. I'm not sure what came over me.'

'I am sure,' he replied. 'Look at me, Reiko,' he rasped huskily. 'Look at me properly and tell me if it's embarrassment I'm suffering from.'

She looked. And swallowed. His fists were clenched on the table, a pulse jumped in his temple, and his whole body was held taut in a grip of an emotion she'd become acquainted with all too well.

He was supremely, spectacularly aroused. From her simple, truthful words. The notion was so intensely powerful, so devastatingly power-drenching she couldn't immediately form adequate words to answer him. 'I…I'm…'

'You're ready,' he stated. 'I trusted you with something important to me. How did that make you feel?'

'Respected. Cherished. Like I matter to you.'

'How do you feel about me? When you look at me, do you see a man who will hurt you again?'

She sucked in a breath. 'Not intentionally,' she replied honestly. 'But—'

He scraped back his chair. 'No more buts.' Without taking his eyes from hers, he reached out a hand.

Tentatively, she placed her hand in his. He swung her up into his arms as if she weighed nothing.

After spending countless hours imagining what his suite, especially his bed, would look like, Reiko barely saw it as Damion kicked the door shut and lowered her to her feet.

He reached for her, sealing her lips with his in another searing kiss that sent her heart rate soaring skyward. Beneath her roaming, frantic hands his muscles warmed to her touch, his skin heating up as their kiss grew more fervid.

But the heat threatened to cool when he reached for the hem of her cotton top.

'I… Do you mind turning the lights off?' she murmured against his lips.

He raised his head and speared her with a direct, probing look. 'Why? I've seen the scars on your face and arms. It's no use hiding them from—'

'Damion, there are more scars—worse scars,' she blurted out, the heat receding to be replaced with the familiar drench of pain.

She tried to step away, but he held her still, his narrowed eyes scouring her face.

'Show me,' he commanded.

'No. We can do this…it…with the lights turned off.'

'I want to see you. Every inch of you. And you won't deny me. Now, do you want to take your clothes off or shall I do it for you?'

His implacable stance made her heart dive into her stomach.

'Damion, please…'

'Every inch. Trust me and take off your clothes.'

He stepped back to give her room, hands locking behind his back as if to physically restrain himself from touching her. That single gesture, the knowledge that he knew she was scarred and still wanted her, made her feel a powerful emotion that lent her fingers the strength to reach for her top.

Grey eyes devoured her the moment she bared herself to him, his gaze lingering longest on her lace-covered breasts. Then he frowned. 'I don't see any scars.'

Taking a deep breath, she caught the long, heavy curtain of her hair and looped it over one shoulder. Slowly, her heart hammering with each passing second, she turned around. Reiko felt his gaze on every single one of the long, livid scars criss-crossing her nape and back. Knew the moment he stepped closer, bringing his forceful presence with him.

What she wasn't prepared for was the slow, almost reverent touch of his fingers tracing her scars. Or the touch of his lips against the deepest scar in the small of her back. Shocked, she glanced over her shoulder.

For the second time today, Damion Fortier was on his knees,

his fingers and lips heating up skin that had gone clammy and tight with dread.

Tears welled in her eyes, a choking sob shaking through her frame. He caught her to him, resting his cheek against her back as she sobbed. Finally he rose and gathered her close, murmuring to her softly in French.

When her tears subsided, he reached for the fastening of her pencil skirt. Fresh dread crept through her. 'There's more, Damion.'

'Every inch, Reiko,' he returned, his deep, purposeful tone brooking no argument.

He eased her skirt down, taking her panties with it. Her bra came off next. Naked, scared and more than a little shaky emotionally, Reiko wanted to bolt. But Damion's eyes held her captive. The harsh breaths rushing from his chest, the volcanic heat of his gaze and the taut control he held over his body made her entertain the belief that maybe, just maybe, he wasn't revolted by the sight of her. The very thought of it made her sway with relief.

He caught her to him, capturing her face in his strong hands so he could devour her lips one more time. His teeth caught her lower lip in a not-so-delicate bite that made liquid heat rush to her core. Against his hard chest her nipples peaked, burning with the urge to be touched. As if in tune with her every need, he captured one breast in his palm, kneading it before squeezing her nipple between his thumb and forefinger.

Against the ravaging force of his lips, she cried out.

With a loud sucking noise, he pulled back. He licked his lips as he stared down at her body, his hand reaching out to capture her other breast.

Her moan was long and loud and desire-drenched.

'Do I still turn you on?' he demanded, his voice harsh with arousal.

Through desire-swollen lips she answered, 'God, you know you do.'

'Do you trust me?'

'Yes,' she breathed.

He grasped her waist and picked her up, his strides long and focused. Gently he laid her on the bed and stood back. He inhaled slowly, his gaze never leaving hers as he stood and released his belt and lowered his zipper. Her gaze started to slide downward.

'Keep your eyes on mine. I need to see the trust in your eyes. And you don't need to see how needful I am for you right now.'

'But you're perfect. I...I'm not.'

'Your scars don't define who you are. Besides, I wasn't talking about that. Five years is a long time, but I haven't forgotten how tight and small you are. I, on the other hand, am not.'

No arrogance, just statement of fact.

The breath rushed out of her lungs. 'Stop boasting, Damion. I know how big you are. I also know you won't hurt me.'

Relief poured out of him. 'You unman me with your words, *ma belle.*'

'Not too much, I hope. I need a bit of your manliness.'

With a grin, he shucked off his trousers and stepped from them. 'My bounce-back rate remains phenomenal.' He stretched out beside her, his face sobering as his graze traced over her. 'I want you. Badly.'

She shifted closer to his warmth, gasping when her breasts encountered the silky hair on his chest. 'I want you, too.' Unable to help herself, she pressed her lips to the tight skin of his shoulder.

A shudder raked his powerful frame. 'Reiko, I need to make sure you're ready. I can take this as slow as you want.' His voice held a gently pleading quality that lit a triumphant flame in her heart.

Boldly, she raised one leg and slid it over his thigh. 'I'm ready. Feel free to check it out for yourself.'

The hand that had been causing havoc with her breasts stilled for a moment, then trailed down over the marred flesh of her stomach, through the silky curls, before dipping into her cleft.

A deep groan tore through his throat at the wet evidence of her need. She lifted heavy lids and her gaze collided with his. With the utmost care, he dipped one finger inside her. Her muscles immediately tightened around him.

'Are you okay, *ma cherie*?' he rasped throatily.

Breath gushing with trepidation, she bit her lip and nodded. There was no pain, but the tightness held a mild discomfort. Damion withdrew his finger but kept his hand pressed against her. His thumb circled her clitoris, sending waves of renewed pleasure roaring through her. Just as he'd done at the pool, he took one nipple in his mouth, his tongue flicking urgently against her flesh, causing her to cry out.

She grasped his silky hair, her movements almost forceful, as wild, unbearable hunger washed away anxiety. Again and again he took her to the edge, only to withdraw before she took that final step into oblivion.

Hot, unrecognisable sounds ripped from her throat. Urgent fingers clawed at his back. Her head thrashed on the pillow as he turned her body into one massive erogenous zone.

'Please, Damion… Oh, please…' she pleaded until she was nearly hoarse.

Finally he bit lightly on her nipple and increased the pressure on her throbbing nub. With a sharp, hoarse cry she felt her orgasm rip through her, the force of it bucking her hips straight off the bed.

She fell back to earth, shaking, moaning, trying desperately to hold on to Damion, her anchor in a rapidly disintegrating world.

It wasn't until she had sufficiently calmed that she realised Damion had two fingers fully imbedded in her. And that there was no pain.

Her shocked gaze locked with his. He leaned down and brushed his lips over hers.

'How do you feel?' His accent thickened his query.

'Fine. I feel…amazing,' she breathed, fresh tears prickling her eyes. She blinked them away and focused on him. Against her thigh, the heavy evidence of his arousal throbbed. 'I want to feel you. Inside me.'

He shook his head. 'Not yet, *ma petite*. You still feel incredibly tight.' He kissed her again. 'I don't want to hurt you.'

'You won't.' She moved against his fingers and watched sweat bead his forehead. When she moved again, he pulled back slightly and pushed into her.

Sensation raced across her skin, setting her on another journey into bliss.

'Damion, please…'

'Not yet, but very soon. I promise,' he murmured against her ear, before proceeding to list all the things he was going to do to her. His fingers picked up a slow but steady rhythm, his thumb circling all the while in an expert motion that drove her insane. 'How does that feel?'

'Good…so good!'

'You look so beautiful. Your body is as incredible as I remember. So responsive and alive with what you're feeling. I've never been this turned on in my life.'

'You…you do it to me.' She clamped her eyes shut as bliss rushed over her. A sob tore through her throat as another powerful climax ripped through her.

She opened her eyes to the sound of ripping foil. Swallowing thickly, she watched him slide the condom on. Unbelievably, anticipation fevered through her. The thought of experiencing a different climax with Damion, after all this time, fired her blood, making her reach out eagerly for him as he sucked in a controlling breath before rearing over her. A flash of concern darkened his eyes.

Reaching up, she pressed kisses along his jaw. 'I'm ready. I promise.'

He swallowed and nodded, his eyes devouring her as he spread her thighs and settled between them.

She looked at his penis, poised against her core. He was so thick and powerful.

He was barely inside her before her muscles started to spasm in protest. Alarm tore through her, her breath emerging in shallow gasps as her fear escalated.

Sinking onto his elbows, he grasped her face in his palms. 'Reiko, look at me.'

She shook her head, every frightened atom of her being ready to reject the forceful presence.

'Look at me, please! Trust me. Feel how much I want you.'

Forcing aside her fear, she looked into his eyes. The strong, steadfast reassurance there slowly calmed her. The soothing caress of his fingers through her hair brought tears to her eyes.

'Relax,' he breathed, placing gentle kisses against her temple.

He pushed again. Reiko felt him slide in another millimetre. A different sensation fizzed through her. Another inch and she felt her heart hammer to an altered rhythm. Slowly, exhibiting infinite care and steely control, Damion fed himself into her. He never once looked away from her, never stopped telling her how beautiful and brave she was.

He established a steady rhythm, pulling out a fraction before sliding back in. This time the connection was more intimate, more visceral, because he kept her in his sights the whole time, gauging her every reaction and devouring the minute gasps that started deep in her throat and gradually worked their way out.

Before long she was clutching his back, her hands feverishly exploring, searching for a different peak from the ones she'd previously attained. Sweat dripped down his jaw and landed on her breast. Reaching up, she slid her hand over her his cheeks and into his hair, the intimate feel of his sweat-dampened hair ramping up her pleasure.

'*Mon Dieu*, I adore your body,' he muttered gruffly.

'Say that last bit again, in French,' she pleaded, the high

of having him whisper throatily to her adding to the insanely heady magic unravelling inside her.

He did, repeating a litany she didn't understand but which, coupled with the expert thrust of his hips, soon sent her over a peak much headier than she'd previously experienced.

'*Merci,*' he murmured in her ear once their breaths had calmed. He gathered her close, tucked her back to his front and pulled a warm sheet over her.

'I think you've got it the wrong way round. I should be thanking you,' she murmured sleepily.

His lips found her sweaty nape. 'Your trust means a lot to me.'

A long time after his steady breathing told her he was asleep, Reiko lay awake, gripped with the terrifying feeling that the only reason she'd allowed herself to trust Damion was possibly because she was falling in love with him.

The next two weeks rushed by in a heady, blissful blur. During the day she stood by Damion's side as he opened the *château* each morning with a short speech before handing the day's tour over to Sabine LeBoeuf.

But once everyone had left, Damion dined with his grandfather, if Sylvain felt up to it, or with her on the terrace. Afterwards Damion would take her to the thermal pool. Sometimes he let her wear one of the bikinis he'd insisted on buying her. Most of the time he preferred her naked—a state she still found a little disconcerting.

The day before the ball, he came to find her mid-morning as she was going over last-minute menu details with the head chef.

'Here—try this.' She forked a piece of lobster with mango-and-lime-infused sauce and held it out to him. He chewed and nodded in approval. 'It'll be the starter, served with a Mersault, then beef or fish for the main. François suggested *foie gras*, but I've convinced him to change his mind.' She smiled at the

French chef, who gave a wry shrug and set out the dessert. 'Do you want to try the dessert?'

His hands arrived on her hips, his body drawing closer to hers. 'Whatever you go with is fine. I trust you.'

Her heart gave another lurch, as it had done lately every time Damion made such comments. And he did it with resounding regularity. She wasn't sure why it frightened her. No. Scratch that. She knew why. She feared she was falling into the trap of believing this thing between them had some sort of healthy shelf life, when deep down she knew it was a fleeting moment in time.

Except with every demonstration of his trust, she felt herself falling deeper into an abyss she feared she might never be able to get herself out of once he learned the whole truth.

She touched François's arm in thanks and felt Damion stiffen beside her. Even before the chef had disappeared back into the vast kitchens, Damion was turning her to face him. The dark look of displeasure on his face stopped her breath.

'What's wrong?'

He pulled her closer until his face was inches from hers. 'This touching other people. It has to stop,' he breathed.

Her mouth dropped open. 'It doesn't mean anything.'

He shook his head. 'It does. It's a coping mechanism—your way of anchoring yourself. The way you did with your father when you were trapped in the crash.' His voice gentled. 'I get it, but you have to stop. I can't handle it.'

'Does that mean I can't touch you, either?' she teased.

The look he gave her scorched her soul.

She sobered. 'I can't help it, Damion. My therapist told me to accept the flaw and use it as a crutch if I needed to.'

His hands slid up and down her sides in a soothing caress but his lips firmed. 'I'm beginning to think your therapist was a quack who should be shot. Reiko, I'll help you cope. Every time you want to touch someone, touch me.'

'And if you're not around?'

He kissed along her jaw and whispered in her ear, 'Just think of me holding you, touching you. Let that be your anchor.'

Intense feeling rushed through her, making her mouth dry and her heart rate soar as she looked into his eyes. His words, the depth of feeling in his voice, all pointed to the impossible. She refused to believe Damion felt anything more for her than mere transient lust. Because anything else would be unthinkable. And yet…

Just like his steady assault on her resistance to sleeping with him, he seemed to be mounting a steady assault on her emotions—almost as if he cared about her…

Completely rejecting the thought for the ridiculous notion it was, she gave in to the kiss she knew would follow.

When he finally lifted his head, the look in his eyes threatened to send her emotions into freefall once again.

'Was there a reason you came looking for me?' she asked, as a way of bringing herself down to earth.

'*Oui*. I have to go into Bordeaux to pick up a painting—a Ventimiglia. You said you had nothing suitable for the ball. I thought we could kill two birds with one stone.'

A memory nudged her mind. When it didn't immediately reveal itself, she shrugged. 'Sounds great. I'll go and finalise the dessert wines with François, grab my bag and meet you out front in ten minutes.'

He nodded, then leaned down and pressed another hard kiss on her lips. 'Remember—no touching.'

'Scouts' honour, Baron.'

His eyes darkened, but his only response was a light tap on her rear as she walked away.

Damion insisted on accompanying her on her shopping trip. He then proceeded to take command of the changing room and dismiss every gown she tried on. It was either too tight or too bold or too sexy.

'You want me to ask the saleswoman if she has a sack in the

back? I could just cut two holes in it to see where I'm going and be done with it,' she teased when he rejected yet another dress.

He rose from the armchair and came towards her. Grey eyes skimmed her from head to toe, and a possessive look devoured her whole.

'I don't want any other men looking at you and getting ideas.'

She snorted, then realised he was serious. 'Thank you...I suppose.'

'You *suppose*?' He caught her to him, hands skimming over her bottom to pull her into his body. 'You don't think other men want you?'

She shrugged, feelings of insecurity rushing back. Pushing them away, she looked at him, at the look in his eyes, and sucked in a deep breath.

'You've given me so much these last two weeks. Much more than I can ever repay you for. I'll always be grateful to you for that.'

'I don't want your gratitude, and I don't like the sound of that little speech. It smacks of *I'm about to dump you*, which can't possibly be the case.'

The lazy assurance as he tugged her into his arms should have irritated her.

Except it was true. She wasn't about to dump him. She would have to eventually. She knew that. But she wasn't ready to let Damion Fortier go. Not just yet...

A discreet cough broke their kiss. Damion laughed beneath his breath, muttered something about this becoming a habit, and they both turned.

Reiko gasped. Damion nodded with approval and almost purred with satisfaction. '*Oui*, that's the dress. We'll take it.'

CHAPTER TWELVE

DAMION STRAIGHTENED HIS TUXEDO and adjusted the gold cuff-links bearing the Fortier family crest. He refused to admit he was nervous. Nerves would mean there was more to the plans he'd made than mere altruism.

He frowned at his mocking reflection and jerked at his sleeve. So, yes, he *did* care.

Reiko would be annoyed, of that he had no doubt, but she was also practical. She would understand the reason behind his actions.

Satisfied with his reasoning, he glanced at the connecting door to her suite and felt the familiar pulse-leap. Although she slept in his bed, she insisted on dressing in her own suite—a decision he disapproved of but one he'd granted her anyway. He didn't dismiss the fact that she needed more time to be completely confident with him. As for her recurring nightmares, the ones he'd arrogantly thought would disappear just because he held her in his arms at night...

Teeth gritted, he walked into her suite.

At the faint sound of her shower, every cell in his body tightened in arousal. With every pump of his heartbeat, he wanted to open that bathroom door. But he knew if he did they'd never make it downstairs in time.

He'd requested his first guest arrive early.

With heavy, reluctant feet, he stepped away from the door and went downstairs just as a car drew up outside. Crossing the hallway, he nodded to the butler, who opened the door.

Again nerves tightened his nape.

But he accepted that big, life-altering decisions warranted a few nerves. The simple fact was that he'd made his decision. And nothing would stand in his way.

* * *

Reiko twirled in front of the mirror, a smile of pleasure lighting her face as she watched the dress flare before falling to rest against her body. She'd fallen in love with the aqua-and-molten-gold dress at first sight. Sleeveless, with amber crystals sewn into the bust, the dress fell from just below her breasts in a gold skirt, with aqua chiffon gathered panels that fluttered with every step. Against her tanned skin, the material felt rich and deliciously decadent. Her hair fell free in its customary long waves down her back, and on her feet delicately strapped gold heels completed the look.

She was glad she hadn't tried on the dress in front of Damion. She wanted to savour the look on his face when he saw it on her. She also wanted him to see her gratitude that he'd helped her regain enough confidence to bare her arms for the first time in nearly two years. She glanced at the long scar on her arm and smothered the fluttering of trepidation.

After one last make-up check, she picked up the matching silk wrap and made her way downstairs.

The muted voices coming from the living room next to the ballroom drew her attention. With a smile pinned in place to welcome this early guest, she entered the room.

Damion turned sharply, came towards her and slid an arm around her waist. 'Reiko, allow me to introduce you to Dr Emmanuel Falcone.'

Despite his easy tone, she detected his tension. She glanced at him, but his face remained carefully neutral.

Pasting a smile on her face, she extended her hand in greeting.

'Dr Falcone is a world-renowned therapist...'

The rest of Damion's words faded underneath the punch of shock that stopped her breath.

Her heart raced, her thoughts scattering, as everything she'd thought these past two weeks had been about disintegrated before her eyes.

'Reiko?' Damion's voice held a tinge of uncertainty as he glanced down at her.

Somehow she managed to find her voice, to answer him and conduct what she knew was a subtle interview with the therapist.

Reiko forced herself to remain calm, but deep inside something cracked, then pain poured through her. After all he'd said, everything he'd led her to believe, Damion believed she was flawed.

Dr Falcone mentioned something about suitable times and appointments. Reiko nodded along and accepted his card, willing the numbness not to overtake her.

What did it really matter? She would be gone from here soon enough.

She finally focused to realise both men were staring at her in silence.

'Um, I need to ring through to the kitchen and check that everything is ready. I'll be out in a few minutes.' Reiko was glad her voice held. Yep, she was still great at keeping up appearances.

After they'd left—Damion casting a puzzled look at her as he escorted the doctor out—Reiko took several breaths, willing the pain away.

Outside, she heard the sound of cars arriving, voices carrying anticipation and excitement at the evening ahead. She could do this…she *could*. And after tonight she'd leave.

Sucking in one last deep breath, she turned.

Damion stood framed in the doorway.

Her heart kicked at the sight of him, then dropped when she saw the intent purpose on his face. 'Not now, Damion.'

'*Oui.* Now.' His nostrils pinched as he inhaled sharply. 'You're angry with me. I know that. But I only wanted—'

Anger flared into being, washing aside the last of her shock. '*You* wanted. So far everything's been about what *you* have wanted. You invited him here without my agreement. Because you still think I'm broken, that I need to be fixed.'

He paled and grasped her hand. 'No, I do not. But I do think you need help to work through those nightmares.'

Weary resignation washed over her. 'I've accepted them as part of my life. Besides, they're not your problem.'

His jaw tightened. 'They shouldn't have to be part of your life. You've been through enough.'

'I really don't want to do this right now.' She glanced towards the door as the voices grew louder.

Warm hands tightened on hers. 'You have to do it sometime. This cannot go on, Reiko.'

She shook her head. He'd made her face a few demons in the past few weeks, but the fear that Damion was gradually taking over her life and her emotions had become a reality she couldn't ignore. If she didn't take care, he would devour her whole.

'Your guests are arriving. I need to make sure they're comfortable. The models are also assembling for the show. That's what you hired me for, after all, isn't it?'

He dismissed her words with a typical Gallic hand gesture. 'The guests can entertain themselves. This is important.'

'You have lousy timing, Damion. All this time you've been determined to set me on the straight and narrow. Now just as I think I could get into this whole organizing-slash-party-planning thing, you want to tear me away.' She shook her head satirically.

His face closed, but not before she caught a look of uncertainty.

'I've messed up. I realise that now. Let me try to fix this.'

'That's just it. Don't you get it? You've been trying to *fix* me ever since we met. And you know what? I think I prefer myself broken. I'm much more fun that way.'

'Reiko, *arrête*.'

She lifted her chin. 'It's also not fair that you can speak

Japanese and I can't speak French. That annoys the hell out of me, actually—'

Her snarky response was choked off in her throat as she looked over Damion's shoulder and caught sight of who'd just walked in.

Isadora Baptiste. Blonde, blue-eyed, statuesque and extremely beautiful, she was everything Reiko knew she would never be. And, as if to drive the point home, two young girls, dressed in similar white gowns to the world-renowned designer's, flanked her. Isadora's children.

In that moment the fact that *she* would never be given the opportunity to experience motherhood for herself ripped a path of pain through Reiko.

'You invited her?' She wasn't sure which emotion reigned supreme—shock or devastation.

He glanced at his old flame. 'Isadora is still a friend.'

She tried to pull herself together, to find the poise and composure that had been sorely missing since she'd walked downstairs and been thrown into chaos.

'Well, let's go and greet your *friend*, then, shall we?'

For the next five minutes, Reiko staged the performance of her life. She sailed ahead of Damion and introduced herself. Although Isadora smiled at her, her attention strayed to Damion, her eyes devouring him in a way that made Reiko alternately want to claw her eyes out and hurry away so they could have privacy. Worse still, all four broke into French, leaving her biting her lip as fresh waves of despair crashed over her.

She withstood it for as long as humanly possible. 'Excuse me.' She pasted on a smile as she excused herself and moved to the next set of guests.

For the next hour, she kept a safe distance. Every time Damion stalked closer, she moved away. Once she caught his eyes across the room. His displeasure hit her like a sledgehammer and a shiver washed over her at the dark promise of retribution. Defiantly, she glared back at him.

What right had he to feel annoyed when he was the one who'd upset her? As Reiko glared, Isadora sidled up beside him and slid her arm through his. Pain scoured through her. He must have caught it because his expression changed. The hint of gentle speculation made her feel even more exposed.

Her heart hammered. Damion learning of her deeper feelings for him was the last thing she wanted. She was already vulnerable enough as it was. Isadora leaned up to whisper in his ear. He smiled but his gaze never wavered from Reiko.

He finally looked away when one of Isadora's daughters, Alaine, tugged on his sleeve. But it wasn't before Reiko knew with every fibre of her being that Damion had seen into her heart, had guessed at her devastation. And had every intention of exploiting it.

She started as a deep voice murmured beside her. 'Here we are again. The *déjà vu* is overwhelming, *non*?' Sylvain Fortier demanded, a shrewd gleam in his eyes.

'Yes. I mean, no.' She cleared her throat. 'Sylvain, it's good to see you again—'

He waved her away. 'Let us do away with the platitudes, *ma petite*. It is time to stop running away.'

'I beg your pardon?'

He nodded to where Damion stood, surrounded by Isadora and her children, his stunning dark looks a perfect foil for their blonde beauty. The perfect picture they made tore a path of pain through her chest.

'You need to stop running and grasp your future before it slips away from you.'

A bitter laugh scoured her throat. 'Nothing in my future includes *him*. I'm here to do this job, followed by another— preferably somewhere far, far away. Speaking of jobs...' She waved to Sabine LeBoeuf, who was trying to catch her attention.

With relief, she excused herself from Sylvain and hurried away—but not before she caught a look similar to Damion's assessing one crossing his face.

'What's going on?'

Sabine fluttered agitated fingers. 'One of the models hasn't turned up. The agency said she was on her way but she's not here, and the show starts in ten minutes. With only six models, the show won't run to time, and the fireworks are set on a timer, so they can't be delayed.'

Reiko tried not to panic. Sabine was distressed enough for both of them. 'Where the bloody hell am I going to conjure up a model at the eleventh hour?' she muttered under her breath.

The stylist approached them, speaking rapidly into his phone. She gazed hopefully at him. When he shook his head, her heart dropped.

'We could ask one of the guests? Madame Baptiste, perhaps?' Sabine suggested.

'No!'

'No…'

The stylist's endorsement of her rejection pleased her. Irrational though it might be, Reiko wanted Damion's ex-lover nowhere near the production she'd poured her soul into.

Her heart stuttered at the speculative look in the stylist's eyes. 'What?'

'I think we've found our solution,' he said.

Relief poured through her. 'Excellent. Who is it?'

'You.'

'Me? Are you insane?'

'You'll be perfect.'

'Sure—in the land of Lilliput. In case you haven't noticed, I'm five-foot-two. Even with three-inch heels, I'd still look ridiculous alongside the models.'

'You'll be perfect,' he insisted.

Sabine clapped in delightful agreement. 'Your make-up is impeccable, but you'll have to wear your hair up—we don't want that lovely mane competing with the Fortier gems. I'll send an assistant to help.'

'Help with what?'

Damion's deep voice sounded just over her shoulder. Heart in her throat, she whirled to face him. How long had he been standing there?

'We had a logistics problem,' she murmured, feeling faint. 'But it looks like it's been resolved.'

'You don't sound sure.'

Of course she wasn't sure. What she was contemplating frightened her. She'd bared herself more in the past two weeks than she had in the past two years. The thought of baring herself to the scrutiny of some of the world's most stunning women and influential men made her blood run cold.

But slowly her heart hammered with determination.

'I am now. I'm sure.' Unable to help herself, her gaze drifted over him. In his exquisitely cut tuxedo, he knocked the breath clean out of her lungs. 'What are you doing here?'

'I wanted to find out what was keeping you.' His gaze probed hers. 'We need to talk, Reiko.'

'I'm not sure what good that'll do.' Seeing him with Isadora and her children had driven home what she could never give him. No amount of talking would resolve that.

'You know me well enough to know I won't take no for an answer.'

She opened her mouth to refute him but Sabine re-entered, flanked by two burly bodyguards carrying glass cases containing the Fortier jewellery.

Damion looked from the pieces to the models, then back at her. 'You're missing a model?' he asked.

'Not any more,' Sabine trilled. 'Reiko has stepped in.'

Several intense expressions flitted across his face. Then his gaze slid to the jewels.

The first piece was a sixteen-inch double-strand necklace composed of endless emerald beads interspersed with twenty-four-carat gold nuggets, each bearing tiny imprints of the Fortier family crest. A matching single-strand bracelet with matching smaller emerald beads shimmered as it was fastened around a model's wrist.

The second model was draped in a necklace of beaten gold shells, the largest of which was centred with a perfect South Sea pearl that glowed under the chandelier light.

The stylist lifted the Grand Duchess tiara from a bed of black velvet. The countless diamonds in the breathtaking design caught a thousand lights as the stylist turned towards Reiko.

'Not that one,' Damion rasped.

Relief weakened Reiko. Just the thought of having so much history weighing on her was unthinkable. The third model, clearly enjoying the honour bestowed on her, preened as the tiara was placed on her head.

A haunting sound of violins signalled the start of the show. A hairbrush-wielding assistant entered and made a beeline for Reiko.

Damion stopped her and took the hairbrush.

'Can I have the room, please?'

Sabine took one look at them and ushered everyone out.

'Sit.' Damion indicated the stool before the lit mirror.

Heart in her throat, she obeyed. His strokes were long and rhythmic, as if he had all the time in the world.

Then he lifted her hair. For the first time in a long time, Reiko felt the whisper of a breeze against her bare nape. She jerked as if Damion's hand had physically touched the three slashing raised scars on her neck. With seductively sure expertise, he secured her hair and reached for a silk-covered case.

He unwrapped it and she gasped. The diamond-and-sapphire choker was the most exquisite piece of jewellery she'd ever seen. Arranged on four strings of diamonds, its centre detail held a sapphire as large as an egg.

The clasp held six miniature stones woven into intricate detail.

He held it up and Reiko's stomach clenched. After he'd adjusted the choker, he pressed a kiss against her first vertebrae. 'Bravo, *ma belle*.'

Tears prickled her eyes. Blinking them back, she forced herself to step away from him. Then immediately stepped back. 'I…I don't think I can do this, Damion. All those stunning people…right next door…and I'm—'

'You're my fearless ninja,' he returned.

She shook her head. 'No, she's taken a vacation. I don't blame her. Even she knows I'm flawed beyond redemption.'

A curious look entered his eyes. 'I disagree. Perfection doesn't exist, but if it did you'd be the closest thing to it.'

'Dammit, Damion. If you make me cry and ruin my makeup, I *will* kick your ass.' She blinked fiercely. 'Anyway, shouldn't you be entertaining your *friend*?'

A smile played about his lips. 'I like that you're jealous.' His eyes fell to the choker and the smile disappeared. 'I like a lot of things about you a little too much.'

With that enigmatic delivery, he pressed a kiss to her forehead and left.

The increased volume of the music interrupted her reeling thoughts. When the stylist stuck his head through the door and asked, 'Are you ready?' every muscle locked in an effort to stay where she was.

Somehow she took a step, then another. At the door, she nodded shakily. 'I'm ready.'

Damion positioned himself at the end of the runway so he'd be the first person she saw when she emerged. He wanted her attention firmly on him. He needed it, craved it. His mind still reeled at the sight of her in *that* piece of Fortier jewellery.

She didn't know the history behind it, of course. Very few did. He suppressed a smile at the thought of her reaction once she found out.

On one side of him his grandfather sat, his gaze focused in front of him. On the other Isadora spoke softly, trying to catch his attention. He didn't feel obliged to give it. His every sense was attuned to the spotlit red velvet curtain, where any moment now—

She stepped out and his breath was strangled in his throat. *Stunning* didn't even begin to describe her. Her head was tilted at a perfect angle to show off the jewellery, her slow, seductive walk striking fire into his loins. He'd had her just mere hours ago, but his body didn't seem to remember its satiation. It screamed his need like a thirsty man screamed for water.

Gasps echoed around him—some with admiration, others with the same puzzlement that sometimes made him wonder just what it was about her that fascinated him so much.

She reached the end of the runway and stared down at him. For a full minute neither of them moved. Her gaze held a hint of fear, a healthy amount of defiance and a whole lot of attitude. But it was the bravery that fired from the core of her being that struck into his heart. Despite the brash exterior, Reiko Kagawa had taken a battering and had come out literally fighting.

He adored her. It was really that simple. He let the feeling infuse his every fibre until he was sure she could see it.

He knew the exact moment she recognised it. Her beautiful eyes widened, her lips parting on a shallow breath that ripped another thunderclap of desire through him.

You're mine, he mouthed.

She saw that, too. Her contact-seeking fingers fluttered against her thighs, brushing the chiffon.

He nodded in silent promise. She inhaled, physically and emotionally gathering herself. Then she turned.

The spotlight fell on her bare back, exposing the myriad scars lining her skin. Another gasp raced through the crowd. Beside him, Isadora's shocked breath barely touched him. He couldn't tear his gaze from Reiko, the feelings rampaging through him threatening to pull him under with their sheer, devastating force.

'If you know what's good for you, boy, pull your head out of your behind and act quickly,' his grandfather grunted.

Damion turned to him and outlined exactly what he intended to do. His grandfather's nod of approval made his heart lift.

He turned and watched Reiko. By the time she disappeared behind the curtain to the sound of thundering applause, Damion knew without a shadow of a doubt that he wouldn't be kissing any more girl-frogs.

Reiko emerged from the cloakroom as the first of the fireworks lit the sky. Despite being shaky from the crowd's reaction, she couldn't stop herself from smiling, or calm her racing, giddy heart.

No one was horrified at my scars. The thought was so freeing she let out an ecstatic laugh. As for the look in Damion's eyes… Heat swirled through her, pinching her nipples and cramping her belly with need.

She would have this one last night. Something to remember him by once she'd left here. It was thoroughly selfish, of course, but right at that moment desire trumped denial.

Sylvain, on his way outside, stopped his electric wheelchair in the vast hallway when he saw her.

'It pleases me to finally see the curse lifted from the Fortier choker.'

Reiko stopped. 'The curse?'

'*Oui.* That necklace was commissioned by my grandfather for his teenage wife. He won her in a duelling match with her intended suitor. And because he didn't want the man to forget, he made her wear it every time they went out in public.'

'Okay, that was…different. But where does the curse come in?'

'She made the Baron's life a misery—just like every Fortier wife who's ever worn it since,' Sylvain explained. 'I can personally testify to that.'

Recalling what she knew about Gabrielle Fortier, Reiko felt her heart go out to him. 'I'm sorry,' she murmured.

Sylvain shook his head. 'Don't pity me. Fortier men might

be prone to loving too deeply, even compulsively, but we love only one for as long as we live.' He looked towards the stairs to where the *Femme sur Plage* had taken pride of place. 'Thank you for returning her to me. Damion tells me you bought the *Femme en Mer*. I think you're not so immune to my grandson as you like me to think?'

Reiko had no words to answer, but as she followed Sylvain, her skin tingled with a different emotion.

The moment she stepped onto the terrace, she felt Damion's forceful gaze.

You're mine.

She didn't resist as he came and pulled her close. They stayed locked together through the fireworks, but with each passing minute her heart sank lower, the euphoric high she'd experienced on the runway giving way to despair.

Damion hadn't been declaring anything special. He'd been putting his stamp on her, proclaiming her as his to the world as if she was some sort of…meat.

She managed to hold it together…just.

The door had barely shut after the last guest before she whirled on him. 'Take this necklace off me, Damion.'

He had other ideas. He swung her into his arms and didn't set her free until they were in his suite. And then it was merely to shed his tuxedo jacket before he snatched her back to kiss her until they both couldn't breathe.

The minute he released her, she stumbled back from him.

'Did you hear me? Take this thing off me.'

His sauntered towards her, dark, sexy eyes gleaming. 'Not just yet. I like it on you.'

'I know why you put it on me. Is that how you see me? As a *possession*?'

He stopped. 'No, but I'm extremely possessive when it comes to you. Watching you tonight…' He shook his head, his accent uncharacteristically thick. 'I hated it every time another man looked at you.'

'Then you should've let me take it off earlier.'

'I was testing myself.'

'What?'

'The first time I saw my grandmother wearing it, she told me the story behind it. Since I knew she wasn't the subservient type, I asked her why she wore it. She told me she wanted to remind my grandfather who was in control.'

Reiko frowned. 'I don't understand.'

'I've never seen a man so consumed by a woman the way my grandfather was with her. She invaded his every living moment. I don't think he took a single breath without thinking of her.'

'Some would call that love.'

His eyes darkened. 'She used his feelings to emasculate him. Is that love?'

'How did he feel when she died?'

'More miserable than I've ever seen him,' he confessed.

She started to tell him what that meant, but a vein of fear struck her heart. 'So this test you were conducting…what was the result?'

His smile was devastating in its power. 'I realised I could breathe.'

Her heart lurched. 'I'm happy for you. Now, can you take this off?'

He didn't honour her request. Instead he took his time to study her. A gleam entered his eyes—one that made her breath catch in her chest.

'Damion…?'

'The diamonds light you up. They caress your neck like a lover's touch.' He moved towards her. 'Like my touch. The idea of someone else touching you makes me slightly insane.'

'I didn't touch anyone tonight.'

'*Non.* Had you done so, we would be having a different conversation right now.'

The hardened, primitive look in his eyes sent a hot thrill of delight through her despite all the warnings she'd given herself.

'Did you spend your whole evening watching me?'

He inhaled deeply. 'That's all I seem to do when I'm with you. It's a compulsion I cannot seem to break.'

Heat surged through her belly, igniting the banked fire that seemed to need just the promise of Damion's proximity to flare to life.

Her hand went to her throat. The sapphire warmed her fingers, the smooth stone almost as seductive as Damion's deep voice. The cloying need to remove it subsided.

'I want you naked—wearing nothing but that choker.'

'Damion...' she murmured, intending to protest, but her voice emerged weak. Her body was already craving him desperately.

His arms banded around her, the heat from his body firing hers up. 'Wear it for me. Let's celebrate the end of the curse.' His hand drifted to her dress and eased the zipper down.

Reiko's protests dissolved under the melting power of his touch. With a soft sigh, she gave in to him. When he saw what she wore underneath—gold-coloured lace knickers—he groaned.

'Or maybe I'm cursed after all. The sight of your body drives me crazy.'

'You're not half bad yourself.'

He growled, picked her up and tossed her onto the bed. She rose on her knees, then reached out to undo his studs. His gaze drifted over her body and she trembled at the fire in his eyes.

Heat pooled between her legs. With urgent movements she slid her panties off. Naked except for the choker, she settled on the bed. Damion's breath hissed out, his hands frozen at his belt. The urge to taunt him further rose inside her. Reaching up, she gripped the pillow and slowly parted her thighs, exposing herself totally to him, this man she realised she'd fallen in love with.

Grey eyes darkened almost to black. The skin around his mouth tightened with the force of his reined-in control, but his hands moved lightning-fast to shuck the rest of his clothes. Gloriously naked, effortlessly beautiful, he sank onto the bed beside her and proceeded to make love to her as if his life depended on it.

Several orgasms later, she woke to find him watching her. She swallowed and felt the subtle tightening of the choker.

'What?'

'I'm breathing, Reiko. You make me breathe. I want you to stay with me.'

A whisper of unease cooled her skin. 'Stay with you? Like… lust bunnies skipping through the fields until they find other lust bunnies to play with?'

His kiss was hard, intending to punish. 'No, there will be no other lust bunnies in your future. Just me.'

'When you say "future", are we talking science-fiction terms or a few seasons of the year?'

'You're getting facetious. Good. Now I know you're listening and taking me seriously.'

Ice clawed at her soul. She had a scary premonition of what was coming. Only Damion didn't know what he was offering. What she desperately wanted to grasp with both hands but knew she couldn't have.

'I want you, Reiko. Indefinitely. You want me, too. This makes sense. I was wrong about the therapist tonight. You're strong enough to work through your nightmares yourself.'

'Damion—'

He stopped her with another toe-curling kiss. 'You don't need to give me an answer right now. You can say yes in the morning.' He kissed along her jaw, leaving a trail of fire that threatened to thaw the ice that had taken hold inside her.

Reiko fought the thaw.

'Listen…'

'Shh. It's scary, I know. I'm scared, too. But we both want this.'

His vulnerable admission tore at her heart. Her love for him increased a thousand-fold. Reverently, she touched his precious face, her heart weeping at the thought of what losing him would cost her.

'Okay. We'll talk in the morning.'

Coward. She pushed the snarling voice away and kissed him. With a groan he took over and kissed her until she wasn't sure whether she was awake or dreaming.

In a daring, desperate move she pushed him down and surged over him. He gasped as she took him in her hand and guided him inside her.

'Mon ange, qu'est-ce tu m'as fait?' His words were choked, fractured, as if held together by the thinnest control.

Flattening her hands on his hair-roughened chest, she rode him, increasing the pace. His head went back, his neck arching as he panted desperate words into the desire-drenched space.

Reiko's senses spun out of control. Strong hands gripped her, held her tight in the emotion binding them, until they could both hold on no longer. Her moans of ecstasy triggered his release. She collapsed onto his sweat-soaked body and felt his chest heave under her cheek. They stayed like that until she was sure he'd fallen asleep.

Tears dripped down her face as she finally raised herself and moved carefully away from him.

Again the choker tightened as she swallowed. With desperate fingers, she searched for the delicate clasps. Several tense minutes later, she finally freed herself from it. She hurriedly placed it on the bedside table, rose and gathered her clothes, determined not to look towards the bed.

Packing took less time than it had taken to remove the choker.

Fighting throat-scouring tears, she slipped her feet into flat pumps and hurried down the hall.

She was halfway down the left staircase when she heard a sound behind her. At the sight of him at the top of the opposite staircase, her suitcase slid out of her nerveless hands and clattered all the way to the bottom. Neither of them glanced at it.

Damion's face was drawn tight, one brow raised in mockery. 'Really, Reiko? I didn't think the middle-of-the-night-sneak-out was your style.'

She swallowed. 'I don't know what my style is. I'm living through a lifetime of firsts with you. H…How did you know I was leaving?'

He held up the choker, his grip tight around its brilliance. 'It slipped and fell on the floor.'

He started to come down the stairs, intense purpose in his eyes. She scurried up her side, overwhelming emotion surging through her.

His brows shot up as he paused. 'Are we really doing this? Chasing each other up and down the stairs in the middle of the night?'

He vaulted up two steps. She dropped down three. Jaw tight with displeasure, he placed the necklace on a ledge and faced her across the large expanse.

'Whatever is making you run, we're going to talk about it. Tonight.' He took a few more steps down.

She hurried up a few more.

He raked a hand through his hair. 'Damn it, Reiko. *Arrête!*'

'No. I can't think straight when you touch me. And I can't let you seduce me into making a decision that you'll regret a few years down the line.'

'Stop talking in riddles and spit it out.'

'I can't be with you, Damion.' Her heart ripped into pieces.

'And I won't let you go. There—that solves the problem.' He pointed a finger straight at her. 'Now, stay put.'

His bare feet slapped the stairs as he surged up towards the landing.

With a yelp she hurried down, only to shriek in earnest when he changed direction. Steadying herself, she changed direction, too.

'You're going to fall and break your stubborn neck!'

With the grace and strength of an athlete, he gripped the

banister and vaulted over it. He landed hard but barely paused before lunging towards her. Within a space of a breath, he was over it and in her face. He tugged her into his arms, gripped her tight as if he'd never let her go.

'First thing in the morning, I'm having these stairs ripped out and replacing them with one staircase.' He pulled back and brushed her hair from her face. 'Now, tell me what's going on. *Now.*'

She shook her head, unable to articulate the depth of her disintegrating feelings.

'I saw you with Isadora tonight.'

'And I saw no one else but *you*. But jealousy isn't what this is about or you'd have clawed my eyes out much earlier. Something's happened. Tell me.'

'Fine. I look at this place and I can smell the history, smell the generations of wealth and power. And I wonder what the hell I'm doing here. I don't belong here.'

'*I* want you here. Which means you belong. Why are you so determined to end this?' His voice was rough.

Looking into his eyes, she felt her heart nearly stop at the fear and a heavy dose of vulnerability.

'Because…because I have to.'

'I understand we're both seriously out of our depths with this one, but walking away is not an option. I won't let you.'

She looked into his eyes and her heart broke. 'I can't be with you, Damion.'

He finally, *finally* seemed to accept that she meant it. His face hardened, his body growing rigid until he seemed carved from stone.

'Tell me why.'

'Because you're the last Fortier. You need to court a suitable baroness, marry her and produce a clutch of dark-haired Fortiers.' Her heart cracked wide open, a shudder threatening to bring her to her knees. 'And I…I can't have children, Damion.'

CHAPTER THIRTEEN

REIKO THREW HERSELF into work as she never had before. Once Yoshi knew of her availability, he tossed dozens of commissions in her lap. She traipsed through dense jungles in Vietnam to retrieve a rare artefact, rode a camel for three days to deliver a painting to a Moroccan sheikh and braved the icy remnants of winter in Kazakhstan to broker a six-piece sculpture deal.

And through it all, no matter how exhausted she got, her last thought at night and first recollection in the morning was of Damion's face after she'd dropped her bombshell.

'You can't have children?'

The blood had leached from his face, his whole body frozen in disbelief.

Numb, she'd shaken her head. 'The doctors told me when I woke from the operation. One ovary had to be removed. The other is damaged beyond repair. My reproductive abilities are less than nil.'

He'd released a shocked breath. Then his lips had parted but no words had emerged. Despite her pain, her heart had gone out to him.

'You do want children, don't you?'

He'd grown paler before giving one grave nod.

Although she'd known the answer, Reiko had felt as if a knife had been plunged into her heart. 'I did try to warn you not to hitch your wagon to this battered post.'

He still hadn't moved. In fact he'd seemed to be reeling from her bombshell. Part of her had wanted to linger, to drink him in one last time. But a major part of her, the part that had been broken and bleeding, had wanted to retreat—fast.

Her fingers had cramped with the need to reach out and touch him one last time. Even in his shocked state, Damion had been so very attuned to her. He'd made a sound in his throat, then *his* fingers had clamped into a fist.

'Goodbye, Damion.'

She'd hurried down the stairs before she lost her nerve. Her battered suitcase had survived the tumble. Snatching it up, she'd rushed through the door. The taxi she'd called from her room as she'd packed was waiting for her.

Her last hysterical thought as she'd been driven away was that she would never get to dance the Argentine tango with Damion…

Reiko let herself into her Kyoto flat and dumped her handbag on the nearest surface. The triple beep of her phone signalled a text. The strong desire to ignore it melted under the thought of what would happen if she gave herself too much free time.

She would end up thinking of Damion, reliving his every smile, his every word, his every touch. And the tears would start again. She, who'd claimed fierce ninja status, had taken to crying herself to sleep most nights.

Typical how your inner ninja deserts you just when you need it most…

Another message beeped. With a sigh, she checked her phone. Yoshi's message was short and to the point.

V.V.VIP client. Commission of a lifetime.

She rolled her eyes and answered. Yoshi's latest client, Tom Radcliffe, had taken a shine to her. Reiko knew she was the reason Radcliffe was sending so much work their way, but deep inside relief bloomed. When she was occupied with other things, she didn't have time to think of Damion.

She hadn't expected him to come after her—the no-children thing would always be a deal-breaker to a man of his pedigree. The Fortier lineage couldn't end just because he lusted after *her*.

Pain lanced through her all the same, the force of it making her gasp out loud. She reached up and released her hair. She'd taken to wearing it up, uncaring of who saw her scars.

She was much stronger now. Because of Damion…

Another tide of misery washed over her. Taking a deep breath, she plunged her fingers through her hair and immediately remembered Damion doing the same beside his pool, his purr of male satisfaction as he'd run his fingers through the heavy mass.

Her phone beeped again. The location of the meeting made her eyes widen. Of all the places in the world… She noted the time and texted her agreement.

Then she sat and stared at her holographic goldfish, willing herself not to dissolve into tears because even *they* now reminded her of Damion.

Cherry blossoms in full bloom in her favourite park in Kyoto normally lifted her spirits, but Reiko couldn't summon up an ounce of pleasure as she chose a bench and tucked her hands deep into her coat pockets. Normally she would have been intrigued by a client who chose such a venue to meet, here in her favourite place in the world, but while her heart was in tatters she didn't much care. On cue, her eyes prickled.

For the love of—

A shadow emerged from behind a particularly stunning blossom tree. The breadth of his shoulders and the arrogance in his stride made her breath catch. She forced herself to breathe.

There was no use suffocating herself over every man whose height or walk reminded her of Damion. Forcibly, she wrenched her gaze from the figure. She couldn't keep doing this to herself. Couldn't…

Her gaze whipped back to the figure.

He was much closer. Close enough to see his face, his eyes, the devastatingly gorgeous cut of his jaw.

Joy slammed through her heart before she desperately wrenched it back.

'*Damion!* What are you doing here?' Her voice, feverishly breathless, squeaked from her throat.

He closed in on her and stared down into her face. 'If you were expecting Radcliffe, I'm sorry to disappoint you.'

Her senses reeled with the reality of him. He'd invaded her thoughts day and night, asleep and awake, for weeks. And now he was in front of her…

She frowned. 'I was expecting Yoshi. And how do you know about Tom Radcliffe?'

His smile didn't quite reach his eyes. 'You walked away from me. I let you because I wasn't at my best. Don't make the mistake of underestimating me, Reiko. Whatever you do, I'll find out,' he promised in a dark purr.

'If that's code for stalking, then you need serious help. And what do you mean, you *let* me?'

His eyes gleamed at her. 'You belong to me, Reiko. It's time to come back.'

Damion watched the different expressions chase over her face, following each one with his heart in his throat, his every sense readying for a fight if that was what it took.

The past three weeks had been the worst of his life. At first he'd told himself she needed time. But it had been *he* who'd needed it.

He'd needed to sift through the disaster zone his hitherto carefully composed emotions had become. In the end it had been simple.

His need for Reiko Kagawa trumped everything else. *Everything*.

'Take a good look, Damion. There's no collar around my neck. You don't own me.'

'I don't want to own you.' He shoved a hand through his hair and paused. 'We belong *to each other*. Putting several thousands of miles between us isn't going to change that fact.' His jaw clenched. 'And letting Radcliffe sniff around you isn't going to make you forget me, either.'

A bleak look entered her beautiful eyes, cutting him to the bone. 'It's not that simple, Damion. You know it isn't.'

He nodded, for a moment unable to speak around the hard thumping of his heart. 'No, it's not easy. But you trusted me with your darkest, most painful secret. And I messed up. I would've come earlier but my grandfather died—'

Her fingers flew to her lips. 'Oh, Damion, I'm so sorry.'

His pain was evident, despite his short nod. '*Merci*. I have no right to ask you to trust me again, but I'm asking anyway. We can get through this, Reiko.'

'There's nothing to get through. I'll never be able to have your children, Damion.'

Pain tore through her as she uttered the words.

His grey eyes darkened. 'Do you want to?'

Her breath rushed out. 'Please, Damion, don't...'

'Why do you want my children, Reiko?' He was relentless. 'I could go first and bare my soul to you right now. But I don't want to frighten you. You mentioned my obsession with you. And you may be right. But I need you to look inside yourself, too. Tell me if what I'm feeling is so different from what you're feeling.'

His words, thick with meaning and expectation, clawed a path of fear through her. Fear of what too much hope might do to her. But it grew, filling the numb place where her heart used to be.

'Why do you want my children, *mon amour*?'

'B...because I love you.'

Damion exhaled, long and hard, then started to move towards her. Just then two small children shrieked past, followed by their heavily pregnant mother.

Time stood still. She wasn't aware she was crying until the chilly breeze froze her tears. Whirling with a sharp cry, she ran.

Damion called out her name but she didn't stop. Couldn't stop. Of course, he was much quicker than her. By the time she arrived at the park's entrance, his SUV was waiting, the doors open. He stood beside it in silent command.

With a resigned sniff, she slid in. All the way to his penthouse, misery gripped her.

She'd told him she loved him. He'd said nothing.

'Do you know this is the longest time we've been in a confined space without you touching me?'

'What?'

'We've been together for over an hour and you haven't touched me once. Do you know how painful that feels to me?'

The low, deep words worked their way through her system to settle low in her belly. His proximity, so seductive, so *touchable*, made her heart ache.

He shut the door and held out his hand to her. 'Come here, Reiko.'

'I…'

'I don't want to tell you how I feel from across the room.'

'How *do* you feel?'

He remained silent, his hand outstretched. Slowly she moved towards him, every fibre of her being vibrating with a tension so strong she feared she'd break in a million pieces. Where normally he'd have lunged for her, he waited for her to come to him.

Finally his hand closed on her. The touch she'd craved and cried out for in the darkness of the night finally arrived.

'I love you, Reiko Kagawa. More than I want children. More than I want to take my next breath. *Je t'aime.*'

Joy burst through her, the depth of her happiness so strong her knees gave way. He caught her easily, strong arms banding around her to lift her into his body. Their kiss lasted until they both needed to draw breath.

Damion leaned his head against her. 'I know my possessiveness frightens you. I'll try to scale it back. I don't know how, but I'm willing to give it a go. Just tell me if you think you're getting overwhelmed and I'll find a way of making it work.'

'How?'

He looked stumped, as if he hadn't thought of the how. And the more he thought about it, the paler he got.

'Damion?'

'I don't have any answers, *mon amour*. All I know is that I can't live a day without you and I pray you'll let me be with you.'

She sighed. 'There it is. The answer I needed.'

A puzzled frown creased his brow. 'What?

'To know that you don't have all the answers. I sure as heck don't. And I like it that way—makes for an interesting life.' Her heart lurched as pain tugged at her happiness. 'Damion…'

'Before you go causing yourself more unnecessary pain, there's something else you should know. I've lined up the best fertility doctors in France. If you want to, we can explore what options we have. If you prefer, we can go the adoption route.'

Her gasp echoed around the room. 'You would do that? But your family…'

'With my grandfather gone, I'm the last of my family. That puts me in the unique position of deciding my own destiny. And I choose you. First and always.'

'You seriously have no idea how hot that makes you to me right now.'

'Hot enough to get naked and sweaty with me?' He nuzzled his way along her jaw.

'For starters. And if you're really, really good, I might even break out the geisha outfit for you.' A hoarse sound escaped him and she let loose a saucy grin. 'Does that turn you on?'

'I've been without you for three weeks. My need is astronomical. So be careful what danger you put yourself in, *ma petite*.' Her grimace made him grin as he skilfully divested her of her clothes. 'You don't like that endearment?'

'When it draws attention to my height and stature? No.'

'You're perfect.'

'I'm five-foot-two. I need stilts just to see half of what's happening in the world.'

He sobered, his gaze intense and deep. 'You have me now.

I'll be your guide. No more stilts for you. I think you've been through enough pain for one lifetime.'

Tears filled her eyes. 'I love you, Damion.'

'Je t'adore aussi. And yes, I'll teach you French.'

'You better. I have leverage.'

'Oh?'

She nodded. 'That painting you picked up in Bordeaux? The Ventimiglia? It's stolen. Interpol have been hunting it for the last six years. The rightful owners are the Busson family.' His complete shock made her giggle. 'Welcome to the dark side.'

EPILOGUE

DAMION WALKED INTO the *château*'s light-filled gallery and stopped dead.

'I think I've just walked into an existential crisis.'

Reiko grinned. 'You poor thing. I could've told you that the day we met.'

He peered closer at the scene in front of him. 'What exactly is going on here?'

'I'm trying to do the Pregnancy Pilates the instructor designed for me. And Stephane is trying his hand at his first abstract painting.'

'But…he's using *you* as his canvas?' Damion's head was tilted to one side as if the better to understand exactly what his three-year-old son was doing.

Her grin widened. 'Don't stifle the process. If pop stars can wear raw meat to express themselves, three-year-olds can paint on their mothers.'

His eyes caught hers, captivated her with the look in them. 'And what do fathers get for suffering through this…horror?'

'They get to join in—after which they may get a special prize.'

The enthusiasm with which he shucked off his shoes and folded his stunning body onto the play mat knocked the breath out of her. Stephane, their adopted son, shrieked his delight as his father lifted him off her back, where he'd been indulging in his mummy-canvas, and tickled him.

Easing herself down from the gentle exercise, she watched Damion. He was the grand prize any woman would kill to win. And he was hers.

She rubbed her hand across her stomach, unable to believe how blessed she was. For two years they'd seen every specialist in France and America. Each time they'd been told their chances of conceiving a child naturally were impossible.

With the adoption process already under way, each blow had felt less painful, until in the end they'd given up altogether.

Then, three months ago, she'd missed one period. Then another. It hadn't been until she'd missed the third that she'd dared to believe. She was too fragile to give birth naturally, and their daughter would have to be born by Caesarean section, but it was yet another challenge Reiko cherished. Just as she cherished her two boys.

'You're giving me the look again,' Damion murmured over their son's head.

'What look?'

'The one that says I'm about to get mind-bendingly lucky—Argentine-tango-style.'

Her laughter brought a lazy, sexy grin to his face. But his eyes drowned her in love and devotion.

Sucking in a breath, she winked. 'Yep, I think you are.'

* * * * *